W. J. Burley lives with his wife in Holywell, near Newquay, and is a Cornishman born and bred, going back five generations. He started life as an engineer, and later went to Balliol to read zoology as a mature student. On leaving Oxford he went into teaching and until his retirement, was senior biology master in a large mixed grammar school in Newquay. He created Inspector (now Chief Superintendant) Wycliffe in 1966 and has featured him in Cornish detective novels ever since, the series has recently been televised with Jack Shepherd starring in the title role.

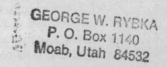

Wycliffe

AND THE THREE-TOED PUSSY

W. J. Burley

CORGI BOOKS

WYCLIFFE AND THE THREE-TOED PUSSY
A CORGI BOOK : 0 552 14205 0

Originally published in Great Britain by
Victor Gollancz Ltd

PRINTING HISTORY
Gollancz edition published 1968
Corgi edition published 1995
Corgi edition reprinted 1995
Corgi edition reprinted 1996
Corgi edition reprinted 1997

This book is set in 10/12pt Monotype Plantin
by Kestral Data, Exeter.

Corgi Books are published by Transworld Publishers Ltd,
61–63 Uxbridge Road, London W5 5SA,
in Australia by Transworld Publishers (Australia) Pty Ltd,
15–25 Helles Avenue, Moorebank, NSW 2170
and in New Zealand by Transworld Publishers (NZ) Ltd,
3 William Pickering Drive, Albany, Auckland.

Printed and bound in Great Britain by

I apologize to the local council and to the planning authority for planting a village of two hundred and fifty people on the coast between St Ives and Zennor without the necessary permits.

I apologize also to the few residents on those beautiful cliffs for saddling them with such obnoxious neighbours.

Of course Kergwyns has no existence outside the pages of this book and neither have the people who live in it.

W.J.B.

Chapter One

Pussy Welles.

Slumped on her plain oatmeal carpet in ultimate relaxation, in the abandoned posture of a child asleep; one arm beneath her body, the other flung out, fingers flexed but not clenched. Her auburn hair shone lustrous in the sunlight, splayed on the pile. Her simple cornflower-blue frock made a splash of colour on the neutral ground. One leg – the right – drawn up under her, only visible below the knee; seamless nylon and a neat, though by no means elegant, flat heeled suede shoe. Her left leg straight and bare, no stocking, no shoe.

The foot was deformed.

Two toes missing, the first and second; obviously a congenital malformation, not a consequence of accident or surgery. All these things ought to have seemed trivial in contrast with the jagged hole between her breasts and the dark red viscous mass clogging the fabric of her dress and the pile of the carpet. But it was not so for the two men who stood over her.

The sergeant was deeply moved by the sight of her deformed foot, a gross flaw where he had supposed only perfection. For the superintendent, it had always been the fact of death and not the means that shocked him; the dissolution of a personality. But they both bent over her in professional scrutiny.

They could not see the wound of exit – if there was one, it must have been hidden by a fold in the material of her dress; but the entry was horrifyingly apparent. They did not touch her; she would have to be photographed, examined and inspected by a gaggle of experts before she was moved. The superintendent looked round the room; all the furniture stood on legs, easy to clean underneath, no draperies, nowhere to lose anything, just an expanse of carpet from wall to wall. The cartridge case lay plain to see against the white skirting board, under a china cupboard.

'An automatic,' the sergeant said, ensuring his credit. 'It looks like a .32.'

'We shall know soon enough.'

Wycliffe wanted to stop the sergeant talking. Soon there would be more than enough talk, an avalanche of facts, fictions, surmises and explanations; for the moment, he wanted to form impressions of his own. He knew the girl's name – at least, he knew what they called her – Pussy Welles. And Pussy Welles was dead, apparently shot through the heart. He could start from there.

As far as he could tell, she must have been about twenty-five or six. He thought her beautiful, and, in death, she had a look of innocence. Deceptive? Why should he think so? Perhaps because a girl is unlikely to be called *Pussy* for her innocence. Feline – but of what kind? I love little pussy, her coat is so warm – that sort? Or green eyed, sleek and stealthy? He could find out by asking the sergeant who was bursting to tell all he knew of the girl, but the superintendent preferred to wait. In any case, he thought he knew already the kind of cat she must have been.

She had money, or at least, she spent it. It was

8

only a cottage, one of those four-square little granite blockhouses with slate roofs that form the nucleus of every Cornish village, but like many of them nowadays, it had been elegantly modernized, gutted and reconstructed from within. This one room ran the length of the cottage and it had two bow windows. The furniture was good quality reproduction stuff – or was it genuine?

Superintendent Wycliffe stood at one of the windows looking out. The little front garden was paved with granite sets and succulents grew in the cracks, sedums and houseleeks. The wooden palings were painted pale blue, a colour which seems to be the badge of those cottages which have undergone their metamorphosis. Beyond, a narrow lane, a stone wall, and the lichen covered roofs of more cottages, grey-green and orange, then the grey square tower of the church rising out of a clump of sycamores just coming into leaf.

A strange spot for the kind of girl she seemed to be. It occurred to him that she was not freckled as most auburn haired people are; her skin was clear, rather pale, translucent. He could swear that she was a natural blonde but what could it matter if she dyed her hair? Most girls do. In any case it would all be in the report.

Deceased met her death as a result of a gunshot wound. The bullet was fired from a Webley .32 automatic pistol and entered the body between the sixth and seventh ribs slightly to the left of the sternum. The wound of entry indicates that the shot was fired at close range, the weapon being held at less than fifteen inches and more than nine inches from the surface of the body . . .

It would all be there, in a wealth of boring detail, essential for the court, if it ever came to court, but very

9

little help in detection. Crimes like this, nine times out of ten, are an explosive result of a build up of tension in human relationships. When those relationships are known, the criminal is known though the technical data may be needed to convict him.

Two men were walking down the lane, dawdling, obviously trying to see as much as possible during their brief passage, unwilling to stop and stare openly. One was heavily built, florid, fortyish; he wore a black polo-necked jersey. The other was younger, slim, small; only head and shoulders visible above the palings, but it was enough; green corduroy jacket, orange cravat; thin, pale, sensitive features, black hair scrupulously parted. He caught sight of the superintendent and looked away at once. As they disappeared down the lane he was gesturing vigorously in conversation with his companion.

Wycliffe smiled. Unlikely that these boys would tangle with a woman!

Her deformed foot was beginning to trouble him, not for the reason it worried the sergeant. The superintendent knew that total perfection is so rare that when it seems to be, one looks the more diligently for flaws. His was a more practical point. Why only one stocking and shoe? Even if she had started to undress in her sitting-room, the other stocking and shoe should be there, and they were not.

He nodded unconsciously in confirmation of a conclusion, having convinced himself that this was a deliberate advertisement of deformity.

A police car came to a halt in the lane, blocking it completely and a second pulled up, hard on its heels.

'They've come. I'm off!'

The sergeant's surprise and obvious disapproval

annoyed him, so that his manner became peremptory. 'Ask the inspector to see that everything is put back exactly as they find it and nothing to be taken away without my permission.'

'Where will you be, sir? – in case the inspector wants you?'

'At the pub – there is one, I suppose?'

Although he was successful, having what is called a distinguished record, he always lost confidence in himself at the beginning of a case; he would avoid his subordinates for fear of sensing their mute criticism, and, forced into their company, he became aggressively dictatorial. Those who knew him shrugged. He'll be all right when he's run in.

Now he escaped through the backway, through a little modern kitchen with a dining alcove, into the garden. It should have been a potato and cabbage patch, hard won from the thin, black stony soil of the moor, but somebody had transformed it into a delightful walled garden with rhododendrons, azaleas, camellias and laurels. Obviously not the dead girl; the garden was made before she was born. A door in the high wall brought him out on to the moor for the house was on the very outskirts of the village. Gorse, heather and brambles grew almost to the door but there was a path of sorts and he reached the lane and made off down it like a guilty schoolboy, away from the police cars. A hundred yards and the lane turned sharp right and on the corner, facing back up the lane, a substantial farm house meticulously cared for; a white gate with a varnished plaque:

Clemens and Reed. Antique Dealers.
Inspection Invited.

Anybody in that house sufficiently interested would know a good deal of what went on in the dead girl's cottage.

The turn in the lane brought him to the square; the church opposite, the pub on his left and a score or so of cottages completing the square. A war memorial in the middle. A pleasant little place, sleepy at this time of year but, no doubt, busy enough in the season.

It was deserted now at any rate but there were plenty of discreetly curtained windows and those who watched, saw him pause, resting on his stick, taking things in. Unless they knew, they would hardly suspect that he was a policeman; he prided himself on that. Barely the regulation height, slender in build, it was difficult to believe that he had ever walked a beat, but he had – twenty years ago. He looked comfortable in his tweeds, not a bit like a bobby off duty. With binoculars slung over his shoulder, he might have been one of the bird watchers who frequented the neighbouring cliffs and coves. But he had no binoculars, just his stick.

Wycliffe never felt like a policeman. Often during his twenty-odd years of service he wondered why he joined. He hated discipline, hated regimentation and sometimes he hated order; but he hated violence more. Perhaps that was why he stayed, but he had joined for no better reason than to get out of the family business. The Wycliffes were large scale market gardeners in Hereford.

Pussy Welles had been murdered; there could be no doubt of that. Perhaps she was not much loss, but violence must never be tolerated. That was his creed. By the same token he was, unlike most of his colleagues, opposed to capital punishment. No compromise! Otherwise you are on the road to Belsen and Hiroshima. For whatever reason he had become a policeman, that was why he remained one.

'Good morning, superintendent, what will you have?'

A modest fame which should have flattered but merely irritated. His answer was surly but the man behind the bar was not easily put off.

Mike Young, licensee, in striped shirt and fancy waistcoat. A heavily built man, running to fat, a high colour and blond, thinning hair. But it was his face which captured reluctant attention. One side of it was a caricature, a series of livid scars from well above the normal hair line down to his jaw bone; the ear pinna was missing altogether and his neck was deeply furrowed by the scars of complex lacerations.

Wycliffe sipped his whisky. There were only two other customers, the two men he had seen passing the cottage. They sat close in the window seat, silent. The older one had a tankard of beer, the other, some short drink, probably gin. Wycliffe had his back to them but he knew they were watching him with interest and apprehension.

'A nasty business, superintendent! Who would want to kill a girl like Pussy Welles?'

'You knew her?' A fatuous question in a village of two hundred people but Young seemed anxious to answer.

'Everybody knew her – and liked her – she brought a bit of life into the place. I'd like to get my hands on the bastard that killed her!' His great thick fingered hands closed convulsively; a man of violence. He picked up his cigarette that smouldered in an ashtray, drew on it deeply and exhaled the grey smoke through pouting lips. Then he leaned forward and lowered his voice confidentially.

'I might as well tell you that the cottage is mine.'

'You mean that she rented it from you?'

The landlord nodded and Wycliffe sensed an embarrassment though he could not divine its cause.

'She took it four or five years back when my mother and father died.'

'Did she have relatives here?'

'Not that I know of.'

Wycliffe filled and lit his pipe, watching the landlord over the undulant flame of the match. 'An odd place for a young woman to settle, a village like this, don't you think?'

Young raised his massive shoulders expressing unwillingness to comment.

'Was the cottage furnished?'

'No, she brought her own.'

'Did you get your rent?'

Hostility and suspicion flared in his eyes. 'I don't know what you mean!'

'I mean did she pay her rent?' The menace in his voice was the more effective in that it was unconscious. He disliked the landlord.

Young reached below the bar for a cloth and began to wipe the polished surface in a reflex action. 'She always paid,' he said sullenly.

A complication here, and Wycliffe thought he could guess what it was. After a prolonged silence, Young looked at him sheepishly. 'I suppose you'll be staying to lunch, superintendent?'

'And I'd like a room for two or three days.'

'I'll go and fix it now.' He was anxious to be gone. Wycliffe detained him.

'As you rented her the cottage, you must know something about her – references – that sort of thing.'

'No, I knew nothing about her, superintendent. She paid me a substantial deposit when she took over and that was good enough for me.' He edged away, like a guilty schoolboy, itching to go before he commits some indiscretion.

'One more thing,' Wycliffe said, 'the antique dealers, what sort of people are they?'

No mistaking relief in Young's distorted grin. He nodded towards the pair in the window. 'You're in luck, superintendent, meet Mr Clemens and Mr Reed.'

Wycliffe took his second whisky to the window and drew up a chair. It was pathetic; they waited for him to speak in frozen attitudes so that he felt like a predator. He introduced himself – superfluous – but it enabled him to be friendly and they responded, tentatively. Harvey Clemens and Aubrey Reed. (Why, for God's sake? – do they change their names when they feel the call, like film stars?). Aubrey was the younger; Nature had played a shabby trick, endowing him with the essential attribute of masculinity when, in all else, he was a woman.

'We know why you are here,' Harvey said.

Wycliffe smiled. 'I suppose the whole village knows by now. Mrs Vines, the lady who found her, will have spread it round a bit.'

Aubrey made an angry gesture. 'She's an old witch! We used to have her to do our cleaning – didn't we, Harvey? – but we had to get rid of her. You don't want to take notice of anything she tells you!'

'I'll bear that in mind,' the superintendent said.

'What do you want from us?' Aubrey was petulant, suspicious.

'Just that your cottage overlooks the dead woman's

15

and you may know who visits her – her friends, if you like.'

'Men,' Harvey said.

Aubrey looked nervously at the bar but the landlord had gone. 'We don't spy on our neighbours, super-intendent.'

Wycliffe let his cold eyes rest on Reed for some time before he spoke. 'Perhaps we should continue this conversation at the police station in a more formal atmosphere.'

Aubrey made a little grimace of shocked distaste. 'We don't want to go to the police station, do we, Harvey?' He put his hands meticulously together and locked them between his knees. 'She had a lot of men friends.'

'Disgusting!' Harvey said.

'Who, for example?'

Aubrey nodded towards the bar. 'He used to be one.' It was obvious that he hated the landlord; equally obvious that he was afraid of him.

Wycliffe refilled his pipe and carefully pressed down the tobacco with a fitting on his penknife. 'Used to be?'

'Until he had that accident. Now, I suppose even she . . .'

'It must have been some accident! – what happened?'

Harvey cut in. 'He was thrown through the wind-screen of his car! Right through the glass! They couldn't see him for blood when they found him.'

Aubrey shuddered. 'Harvey! He was driving home from St Ives late at night, and his car skidded on a patch of oil.'

'Oil?'

'Yes. A five gallon drum of oil all over the road. They think it must have fallen off the back of a lorry or something.'

'He was drunk,' Harvey said.

'Anybody else?'

Aubrey kept his hands tightly locked and swayed gently from side to side.

'There's Dr Barnes,' Harvey said. 'He's a lecturer in archaeology at the University. They've got the cottage going down at Kitt's Cove.'

'They?'

'He and his wife; they spend their vacations down here.'

'Are they down, now?'

'He is,' Aubrey said, 'I saw him yesterday.'

The superintendent lit his pipe and puffed until it was drawing to his satisfaction. 'Did you happen to notice anyone going to the cottage yesterday?'

Aubrey considered. 'Yesterday we worked all day . . .'

'Worked?'

Mild contempt. 'In our showroom. We are dealers in antique furniture and *objets d'art*.'

'And your showroom?'

'Is round the back of the house, a converted barn, so we couldn't be expected to see what went on.'

'But you didn't stay there the whole day, surely?'

'Until the light went.'

'And then?'

'Well, we couldn't see anyone then, could we?' Harvey giggled. He had the same infuriating pertness as Alice's March Hare.

'As a matter of fact it was dark when I saw Barnes,' Aubrey volunteered. 'I was out with Abélard.'

'Abélard?'

'Our pussy. We had him neutered, you see,' – from Harvey.

'One of us takes him out for a few minutes each night before going to bed.'

'And you saw Barnes – where?'

'At the cottage. That's what you wanted to know about, wasn't it?'

'Going in or coming out?'

'I don't know; he was standing on the step.'

'At what time was this?'

Aubrey considered. 'A little after ten. I remember the church clock striking just before I let Abélard out. By the way, what happened to her cat? Is somebody looking after it?'

'You mean that Miss Welles had a cat?'

'A silver point, like Abélard; a magnificent animal.'

Wycliffe suddenly wearied of the precious pair; they were even less prepossessing in their new found confidence than when they were scared. Did they think they were hiding the obvious? Or that he cared?

It was quiet, peaceful. The sun shining through the fake bottle glass windows made intricate green patterns on the marble table tops and on the floor. Now and then he could hear the *ping* of the shop doorbell from right across the square. Half past twelve. A turn round the square before lunch.

He walked in the sunshine. Gulls soared overhead in the faded blue sky and he could smell the sea. A lane ran down beside the inn, the entrance marked by a finger post:

Footpath to cliffs. Residents' cars and callers only.

Select. He would have liked to walk within sight of the sea but it would probably take too long. The six months since his appointment to the regional squad, after twenty years in the Midlands, had not accustomed

18

him to having the sea always round the corner. Instead, he walked by the churchyard. He looked idly at the headstones, slabs of slate, deeply incised with the vital history of the parish and crusted with mosses and lichens. Even the preposterous later crosses and curbs were achieving a decent obscurity. He wondered whether the mortal remains of Pussy Welles would find their way to this consoling place, there to decay in peace. A Mini car shattered the silence, coming into the square; it made its way down on the opposite side of the central green and pulled up outside the inn. He stopped to watch; a young man and a young woman got out, slammed the doors and went through the bar entrance.

He wondered about the village children. Where were they? There seemed to be none; evidently a tidy and well ordered little village. On the surface. He reached the shop and went in to buy tobacco, aware that he was interrupting a discussion. Three women with shopping bags watched him being served and he was certain that the little hole of silence he had made would soon be healed.

A hell of a way to conduct an inquiry, strolling around like a tourist! But he completed the circuit of the square and arrived back at the inn. The bar was empty so he found his way to the dining-room. Three of the tables were laid and the couple from the Mini sat at one. Again he knew that he was interrupting something – a quarrel this time. On closer inspection, they were not so young; little short of thirty, either of them. She was fair, petite, determined; he, mousy, a little blundering and anxious. They avoided each other's eyes, and his.

He sat at a table laid for one.

The waitress, a sluttish young girl in a black dress too tight for her, went to the couple's table. 'Soup for you, Dr Barnes?'

Dr Barnes.

Wycliffe went back to the cottage in a mood of acute depression, with no relish for the tasks ahead. A young constable standing disconsolate outside the door saluted.

'Inspector Darley is inside, sir.'

'Alone?'

'Yes, sir.'

Wycliffe nodded. 'You can get back to your duties. No need to hang about here.' He hated the least semblance of military routine.

Since his appointment he had come to terms with Inspector Darley. The two men had complementary qualities. Wycliffe was imaginative, impatient of routine, inclined to be lazy. Darley followed the book, believed that every one of the twenty-four hours was made for work when there was work to be done, and was never bored. Even physically they were extremes, Wycliffe was slight, almost frail; Darley a giant, bulging in his clothes. All of which scarcely added up to any liking between them.

They talked in her sitting-room but she was gone. The place where she had been was marked with a black outline of her recumbent form and by the rust brown stain on the carpet.

'Anything to tell me?'

Darley spoke with ponderous slowness, his words, like his movements suggested a film run at reduced speed. 'Dr Slade thinks that she died between half past nine and eleven – off the record, of course.'

'No sign of a gun?'

'No. It was a .32 automatic but you probably know that already. There are eight licensed weapons of that description in the division and they are being checked but nobody in Kergwyns has a licence for a .32.'

Wycliffe filled his pipe and passed the pouch to Darley. 'Any indication as to why she should settle in a place like this?'

Darley paused in the act of thumbing down the tobacco in his pipe and stared at the bowl. 'In a way. The local sergeant knows the story. Apparently she arrived in St Ives about five years ago with her husband . . .'

'Husband? – Never mind, I just hadn't thought of her with a husband.'

Darley ignored the interruption. '. . . a man called Horner, Arthur Horner. He leased a shop with a flat over and they set up in business – fancy goods, post-cards, paperbacks, that sort of thing.'

'What happened?'

'Happened?'

Wycliffe snapped. 'Well, she's not there with him now, is she?'

'He died six months after they took the shop.'

'Oh? What did he die of?'

A hint of a smile. 'Falling over a cliff.' Darley had the satisfaction of seeing that he had made his point.

Wycliffe thawed. He sat himself in one of the fragile armchairs. Darley remained standing, discomfort and efficiency went hand in hand in his opinion.

'Accident?'

'So it seems.' Darley re-lit his pipe. 'She had nothing obvious to gain by his death and she wasn't there to push him anyway. All they had was the stock and furniture and that was sold to pay the rent.

'After the husband died, she came here and started to use the name of Welles. I gather there was a convenient arrangement with the landlord of the inn who owns this cottage. Since then there have been other men – according to the gossips.'

Wycliffe sighed.

Darley frowned. 'What a way to live! An attractive young woman, still in the twenties.'

But Wycliffe thought – What a way to die! An instant of violence cutting off a life. Like dropping the curtain at the beginning of the second act. How he hated violence! But Pussy Welles was dead and nothing would bring her back. How many in the village took satisfaction in that fact? For how many of them was her death a reassurance? For which of them was it a desperate necessity? His job to find out.

'What about relatives?'

Darley frowned. 'A girl of her age must have close relatives but there's nothing to show that she was in touch with them. Of course, I've arranged to follow up what leads we've got.'

'Letters, papers, bills . . . ?'

The inspector jerked the stem of his pipe upwards. 'There's a sort of study or office next to her bedroom but somebody got there before us – the killer, I suppose. All her stuff has been tumbled out from the desk. There's no way of knowing what's missing but it's unlikely to be anything of intrinsic value; she had a few bits of jewellery and there was thirty pounds in cash in the desk.'

'It's pretty obvious she lived by her wits and it's possible she was going in for a spot of blackmail.'

Wycliffe drummed his fingers on the arm of his chair. He looked at the chalk outline and saw vividly, for a moment, a mind image of the girl lying there; her slim bare leg outstretched, her deformed foot. 'Did you find her other shoe and stocking?'

Darley shook his head. 'Certainly not the shoe. I don't know about the stocking, there's a drawer full of them up there and they all look the same to me.' He smoothed a massive hand over the broad shining band of baldness that parted the greying vestiges of his hair. 'There were scratches on her thigh, high up where the suspenders fasten to the stocking top, as though somebody had ripped the stocking off with considerable violence.'

'Before or after death?'

'After, Slade thinks.'

Wycliffe was accustomed to Darley's habit of telling the story in his own way. He was perfectly capable of discussing a case for ten minutes before producing a crucial piece of evidence linked to some private theory.

Wycliffe nibbled. 'What are you suggesting?'

'I wondered if this could be a sex crime.'

'Sex murder by bullet?'

The inspector shrugged. 'No, I agree, it doesn't make sense.'

'All the same, those scratches are very odd, coupled with the missing shoe and stocking. As soon as you get Slade's report let me know.'

While he sat, discussing her murder as though it was an academic exercise, Pussy Welles' body would be lying on a slab in the pathologist's laboratory, subject to every conceivable indignity, just to provide the report he mentioned so casually. He stood up, walked to the window, and stood with his back to the room. The sky had clouded, smoky clouds from the south-west billowing overhead drizzled rain. Every last trace of colour drained from the landscape, nothing left but shades of grey. He pushed open the window and let in the moist air that carried with it the tang of the sea.

'Well! Let's take a look up there.'

On the narrow stairs Darley had to turn sideways at the bend and the treads protested. There were two rooms, a bedroom with a window facing the village and a study with its window overlooking the moor. The bedroom was simple, cheerful, and in good taste. A double divan bed neatly made up, a candy-striped bedspread, white walls with prints and a whole wall of floor-to-ceiling cupboards with white sliding doors. A chair, and a minute dressing table with an oval mirror fastened to the wall. A room, chaste in its functional simplicity.

The study was smaller, hardly room to move about. A desk, a chair, shelves crammed with books and a record player with a stack of records. The superintendent glanced over the shelves, modern novels, poetry, books of reference and the records were highbrow too.

'She must have been intelligent and educated,' Wycliffe said. 'You don't associate this sort of thing with a woman who lives as she seems to have done.'

Darley grunted. 'I don't know why not! It isn't a question of education but of morals.' He was a lay preacher when he could spare the time. He pointed to the record player. 'When our chaps went over the place the little red light was still on. It looks as though she might have been playing it when her visitor arrived.'

'The bed was undisturbed?'

'Made up as you saw it.'

Wycliffe lifted the lid of the record player. The top record of a stack was an LP of Verdi's *Nabucco*. It was possible that she died while her cottage was filled with the ineffable sadness of the slaves' lament.

On the writing desk there were two neat piles of papers and the empty drawers were stacked on the floor. Wycliffe shuffled among the papers and was surprised by what he found – a small pile of crossword blanks with handwritten clues. He saw that they were difficult – the academic kind that appear in the more expensive Sunday papers and literary magazines. The other, a pile of quarto sheets closely written in her neat script.

'She's writing a novel!'

'Apparently.' Darley was unimpressed. 'This was all; it was scattered about. I had it collected together and sorted but nothing has been taken away. There doesn't seem to be much that's useful; no engagement book, no addresses or telephone numbers, no letters, no bills even.'

Wycliffe picked up the pile of manuscript, fascinated by the new twist it gave to his ideas on Pussy Welles. By the end of each murder case he was impressed and a little repelled by the extent of his knowledge of the victim, for he seemed to know more of the dead than of the living. And it was beginning here. The personality of Pussy Welles was growing and taking shape in his mind. Five hours ago he had never heard of her; then she was the victim of a shooting, just another victim – no more than an outline, like the outline of her body on the carpet. Seeing her had filled in some of the detail; she was young, good-looking – beautiful, he thought – and she had a deformed foot. She lived in a well appointed little cottage which she had furnished in good taste. Then people began to talk to him about her, telling him that she was a widow, hinting that she lived by her wits, that she was a woman belonging to men. The kind to get herself murdered? Now he had more facts which hardly seemed to fit; she had been well educated, sufficiently so to contrive sophisticated crossword puzzles and to write a novel.

'I'll take this with me.'

Darley raised his eyebrows. 'Here's her birth certificate – Anna Patricia Holst. Her father was of Austrian birth, naturalized British, a musician. She was born in Colchester.'

'If she married a chap called Horner, where does the name of Welles come in?'

Darley shrugged.

'No marriage lines?'

'No. From what I hear she was a bad lot.'

Darley believed that immorality was a disease of the pubic region and Wycliffe was irritated. He found the girl's room deeply moving, an horizon in her life which she could not have known to be her last.

'An inclination to ring the changes in bed doesn't render a girl eligible for murder!'

'I'm aware of that, sir!'

'I suppose you've laid on a house to house?'

'Thomas, Evans and May have been at it since before noon. They're taking their time about it!'

'What sort of brief did you give them?'

Darley raised his massive shoulders. 'The usual. Anybody seen in the vicinity of the cottage last night; anybody who heard a shot; and – more discreetly – who were her regulars?'

'A blank cheque for gossip,' Wycliffe grunted. 'You'll be lucky if they finish tonight!'

Darley was nettled. 'It has to be done, sir!'

The doorbell startled them.

'That'll be them now. I'll go down.'

Wycliffe went to the window. He could not see anyone at the door because of the porch but he stared gloomily across the cottage roofs to the church tower. The drizzle had turned to rain and the wind was freshening; the grey granite, crumbling under encrusting lichens, seemed to soak up water like a sponge. He heard voices downstairs but not those of the detectives; then Darley's heavy tread on the stairs.

'It's a Mr Lomax; he thinks ge's got something to tell us.'

Probably some village crank anxious for notoriety but in a murder case everybody has to be heard. He went down to find the man perched on the edge of a chair, his mackintosh dripping on to the carpet. In the forties, lean to the point of emaciation, studious looking – an impression helped by the thick lenses of his spectacles. He looked about him nervously with quick, bird like glances. Every now and then his eyes rested on the tell-tale chalk marks, but only for an instant.

'Your men came to see me but I thought it would be better if I talked to whoever is in charge . . .' He peered from the inspector to the superintendent.

'Superintendent Wycliffe,' Darley introduced.

'Thank you. It seems dreadful to come here – almost ghoulish, but there is no police station in Kergwyns and I did not know how else . . .'

'You were perfectly right to come here if you have something to tell me.'

Lomax could not settle his gaze, nor apparently, compose his thoughts.

'Perhaps you should begin by telling us who you are,' Darley suggested.

'Who I am? Yes, of course. My name is Edgar Lomax and I am a naturalist, a student of animal behaviour. At one time I was a lecturer in the subject in the University of London.' He spoke with a certain pride. 'Then I came into a little money and resigned my university appointment to pursue my own work with greater freedom – that was when I came to Kergwyns.'

'So that now you are independent, and very nice too!' Wycliffe wondered when he would get to the point.

Lomax nodded. 'In a manner of speaking, yes. With the income from my books I manage very well. Natural history is big business these days and there seems to be an insatiable demand for articles and books at the popular level. It pays for my more serious work and I am able to live very comfortably.' He produced a large white handkerchief and mopped his forehead free of the little droplets of water that drained from his saturated hair.

He looked like a starved, nervous and very wet rabbit.

'You were acquainted with Miss Welles?'

'Yes, indeed. Certainly we were acquainted.' He seemed distressed but marshalled his courage to come to the point. 'This is a small village, superintendent, and we live, so to speak, in each other's pockets. No secret is a secret for long. You will probably know already that Anna – Miss Welles – had a certain reputation where men were concerned.' He paused, as though waiting for confirmation but Wycliffe was silent and he continued, picking his words with care. 'She had a very rich and many sided personality and you will find that she had many friends . . .' He hesitated, then added, 'most of them, it is true, were men, but not all of them were on the same . . . ah . . . footing. I was a very close friend . . .'

He was obviously trying to say that he didn't sleep with her.

'I was, to a certain extent, in her confidence, and I have been aware for a week or more that she has been worried. She admitted as much, and although she did not tell me the cause of her trouble, I gathered that she needed to raise a sum of money.' He coughed uneasily. 'I told her, of course, that she could count on me but she wouldn't hear of it. "No Edgar," she said, "you owe me nothing, but there are those who do." '

He stopped speaking with obvious relief and sat, staring at the toes of his heavy shoes, caked with mud.

Wycliffe thought he understood the man; nervous, sensitive, inhibited, he would revel in the friendship of an intelligent woman with a reputation for reckless living. Playing with fire without much risk of getting burnt.

'You don't know precisely, Mr Lomax, what it was that was troubling Miss Welles?'

He looked up, startled. 'No! Indeed I do not – I wish I did!'

'And you have no idea what she meant when she said that there were others who owed her something?'

Lomax locked his fingers together and regarded them intently. 'I suppose that she meant there were people who owed her money, but I have no idea who they were.'

'When did you last see her?'

His answer came promptly. 'The night before last.'

'The night before she was killed?'

He nodded. 'That was when she admitted to me that she was worried and I offered to help . . .'

'You visited her here?'

29

'Oh, no! We met at the Dampiers' – I walked home with her and it was then that she told me.'

'These Dampiers were friends of hers?'

'Yes. John and Erica, brother and sister, they have a house beyond the inn.'

'Tell me about them.'

Lomax looked puzzled. 'About the Dampiers?'

'If you will, Mr Lomax. We have to get to know as much as we can about this young woman and we can do that best through her friends.'

Lomax accepted this rather specious explanation. 'Dampier writes children's books and his sister illustrates them. They are an accomplished pair, but he is a cripple, poor fellow – a hunchback. He goes out very seldom and he is dependent for his social life on a few friends who visit him for a game of Mah-Jongg and a chat.'

Mah-Jongg! It sounded pleasantly nineteen-twentyish – ragtime, ear-phones and all that.

Wycliffe started to fill his pipe, after offering his pouch to Lomax who said that he did not smoke.

'This little village seems to have more than its share of talent. The Dampiers, yourself – author and naturalist . . .' He puffed strongly, persuading his pipe to draw. 'Then, I gather, Miss Welles made up cross-word puzzles for publication.'

Lomax smiled. He was more relaxed. 'She did indeed, and very good ones. The Dampiers put her on to it, they seem to have a great many contacts in the newspaper and publishing world. As to the rest, I suppose that Kergwyns is typical of many villages in this county, a refuge for intelligent cowards.' He laughed. 'A place where it is possible to hide from the harsher realities of life in the second half of our century; to pretend that they do not exist, or to write about them with an Olympian detachment.'

'Was Dr Barnes one of your Mah-Jongg party?'

Lomax looked surprised. 'Dr Barnes? No, he was not. It is true that he and his wife sometimes come along when they are down but they are not regulars and I doubt . . .' He broke off. 'What made you ask?'

'Who else was at the Dampiers' that evening?'

Lomax was nettled by the new brusque note of interrogation and his manner became constrained. 'Our usual party; in addition to the Dampiers, Anna and myself, there were Harvey Clemens and Aubrey Reed, the antique dealers, and the Mitfords.'

It was not necessary for Wycliffe to speak, only to raise his eyebrows and Lomax went on: 'A couple who live in the village; he is a teacher at a school in Penzance. A keen sportsman, he used to be an amateur rally driver.'

'You are being extremely helpful, Mr Lomax,' Wycliffe said. 'It is essential for us – strangers – to be able to fill in the background and you are greatly simplifying our task.'

Silence while the two policemen smoked and Lomax looked round, a little reassured.

'You said just now that Miss Welles had friends – what about enemies?'

Lomax drew in his thin lips. 'Enemies! – that is being a little dramatic, surely? Most people don't have enemies and I don't suppose she had . . .'

'She was murdered, wasn't she?' Darley snapped and put Lomax off his stroke; his eyes went furtively to the chalk marks once more.

'Yes, of course, it's difficult to grasp. Obviously she had an enemy but it's almost impossible to believe that someone would do such an awful thing. There were some who disliked her but . . .'

'Who, for example?'

Lomax smiled faintly. 'Women in general, I suppose.'

'Men?'

Lomax shifted uncomfortably in his chair. 'I think there was some trouble between her and Aubrey Reed . . .'

'The antique dealer?'

'Yes, they certainly quarrelled.'

'But she still played Mah-Jongg with him at the Dampiers' on the night she was killed?'

'Oh, yes, nobody would do anything to upset that, it was an institution.'

'Have you any idea what they quarrelled about or when?'

Lomax sighed. 'It was quite recent – within the last two or three months at any rate, and I think it was about their cats.'

'Cats?' Darley was incredulous.

Lomax seemed to apologize for human follies. 'You know how these things are. They both have male Siamese but Reed's is neutered while hers is not – she says that she wants it to enjoy the simple pleasures of life. Anyway like many Siamese males it is aggressive and there were fights in which Reed's cat got the worst of it.'

'Hardly motive for murder!' Darley remarked scathingly.

'You evidently don't know many cat owners,' Wycliffe muttered.

Lomax looked round vaguely. 'That was one of the reasons I came over – somebody will have to feed and look after him . . .'

'I have't seen a cat about the place, have you, Darley?'

'No!' With emphasis.

'Odd, but cats are strange creatures, I expect he'll turn up. If so, perhaps you'll . . .'

'Yes, of course, we'll let you know.'

They all seem more concerned about the cat than the girl.

Lomax still had something he wanted to say but found difficulty in saying it; finally, it came: 'You don't think she might have committed suicide?'

'Do you?'

He was taken aback. 'It seems so much more likely than murder.'

'What about the gun?'

'Somebody could have taken it.'

'Who and why?'

A trace of irritation. 'How should I know? But it could have been somebody's gun, somebody who came in and found her and didn't want to be involved.'

Wycliffe nodded. 'An interesting suggestion.'

Another silence.

'Is that where . . . ?'

'Yes, that's where we found her, one leg doubled up under her, the other outstretched.'

'You know when she was killed?'

'Somewhere between nine and midnight.'

Lomax stared at the black outline, openly now. He shuddered. 'Horrible!'

'She was shot at close range from the front, the bullet passed right through her body, penetrating the heart and damaging one of the great vessels. That accounts for the effluxion of blood. You can see it on the carpet.'

Darley looked at his chief in astonishment and Lomax

was pale but Wycliffe seemed not to notice. 'After shooting her, the murderer started to undress her.'

'Undress her?' His voice was little more than a whisper.

'Yes, he tore off the shoe and stocking from her left leg with considerable violence, lacerating and bruising her thighs.'

'Horrible!'

'Yes, murder at close quarters is rarely the cosy business we read about in detective stories. Incidentally, her left shoe and stocking have not been found . . .' He stopped, as though struck by a new idea. 'By the way, Mr Lomax, can you account for your movements last night?'

Lomax winced. 'I was at home all the evening.'

'Alone?'

The wretched man nodded, then he brightened. 'At a little before ten, I rang Dampier.'

'Did you speak to him?'

'I spoke to his sister, she said he was out.'

They were interrupted by the telephone. Darley went to the porch to answer it and they could hear his side of the conversation. 'Yes, he's here, I'll ask him to come to the telephone.' His great moon-face peered round the door. 'It's for you from Dr Slade.'

'I must go,' Lomax announced. He seemed to welcome the chance and pushed past the superintendent on his way to the telephone. 'If I can be of any further help . . .'

Wycliffe watched him go out into the rain, then picked up the receiver. 'Wycliffe here.'

'This is Slade. That girl was pregnant.' The pathologist never wasted words.

'How long?'

34

'Eight or nine weeks.'

'So that she would have known?'

'What do you think?'

'Anything else?'

'Nothing you don't already know.'

'Right, thanks for ringing; the information may be useful.'

'We do our best,' Slade said and rang off.

Darley was gloomily complacent. 'These girls really ask for it!' He was more concerned to discover why Wycliffe had been so brutal with Lomax but the superintendent was enigmatic.

'It was just an experiment and he'll get over it.'

Chapter Two

Wycliffe could not sleep and by seven o'clock he was standing in the doorway of the inn smoking his first pipe of the day. Sylvie, the girl who had served his meals the day before, was already at work, cleaning up the bar, slow moving, her eyes still clogged with sleep. She had taken pity on him and made some coffee.

'Do you know who did it?'

'No. Do you?'

She rested her plump bare arms on the bar counter and wrinkled her brow. 'I'll tell you one thing, it was a woman.'

The superintendent sipped his coffee and said nothing.

'They had it in for her and no wonder!' She ran her fingers through a tangled mop of brown hair, sweeping it back from her eyes. She looked like a child newly awakened. Later in the day when she had done herself up she would look coarse, vulgar. 'No man was safe from her.'

'Good coffee!' He emptied his cup and she refilled it. 'You didn't like her?'

Screwed up features. 'I didn't have anything against her; it takes all sorts, I suppose.' She paused. 'But she wasn't a snob which is more than you can say for some of 'em round here.'

Wycliffe disliked leading the girl on, imposing on her

youth, but a policeman has to get his gossip from somewhere. Oddly, in his old city division, he had questioned scores of girls younger than Sylvie, expecting them to be wise in the ways of vice, surprised to discover occasional innocence. Here in the country it was different, Sylvie reminded him of girls in the village where he had grown up. 'Was your boss one of . . . ?'

Sylvie nodded. 'Before my time – years ago. Not since his accident.'

'So she drew the line at that.'

She laughed. 'You don't know much about women, do you? It wasn't her who laid off, it was him. I know that for a fact. In any case, what are a few scars compared with a humped back?'

'A humped back?'

'Dampier, or haven't you got to him yet?' A malicious grin. 'His sister, Erica, doesn't like it one little bit!' she added in a travesty of refinement. 'That sort make me sick!'

How old was this girl? Eighteen? Nineteen? Certainly no more, yet she treated him like a schoolboy.

'Sylvie!' The landlord stood at the entrance to the bar. He wore his pjyama tunic tucked into the top of a pair of greasy flannels; he was unshaven, unwashed, bleary eyed.

'Good morning, superintendent.' His acknowledgement of Wycliffe was perfunctory. 'Sylvie, it's time you started on the breakfasts.' He evidently disapproved of their tête à tête.

'OK. I'm coming!' She winked at Wycliffe and waltzed off after her employer.

So Wycliffe stood on the steps of the inn alone, smoking his pipe, waiting for the village to come to life.

A better day; the rain had gone with the night and the sun was up, behind the church; the sky was powder blue. Too good to last. He heard a milk lorry rattle along the road a quarter of a mile away and he persuaded himself that he could hear the sea. With more than an hour before breakfast, he decided to go and take a look.

Down the lane beside the inn there were a few more cottages then four or five large bungalows, nineteen-thirty vintage, their gardens choked with *Senecio* and *Olearia*. Each gate displayed a little card with the name of the occupier. There was one for *Mr and Mrs A. Mitford* and the last one read, *John and Erica Dampier*. He could see nothing of their bungalow except the roof from the lane but on the sea side, a huge dormer window topped the grey-green jungle of their wind-break. The ground shelved a couple of hundred yards to the cliff edge so the window commanded a panoramic view of the coastline, all the way from Godrevy to Pendeen. It was too perfect to be real, the sun glittering on the water, the white lace of foam at the foot of the cliffs, the golden gorse scenting the air. He stood on the cliff edge and looked down at the inshore water, a little sinister under the precipice of rock. As he watched a seal bobbed up, then another and another, he had never seen seals before except in zoos. He was so absorbed in watching them that at first he failed to notice a more singular phenomenon closer at hand. A little to his left, a precipitous path led down to a tiny cove, a broken, crumbling, and in the superintendent's opinion, totally impracticable path, but a man was scrambling up, a contorted figure, moving with furious energy, using his hands and arms almost as much as his legs and feet. Every now and then he would look up, presumably to gauge his progress and Wycliffe glimpsed a black bearded face, striking even at that distance, by reason of the high domed forehead.

So Dampier took his exercise in the early morning, presumably to avoid an audience. Poor devil! And what exercise!

Wycliffe would have walked away to avoid thrusting himself on the man in these circumstances but glancing back to the bungalow he could see the form of a woman at the upstair window, watching, and for some reason he felt that it would be cowardly to retreat. In a surprisingly short time Dampier reached the top and stood for a moment, panting and mopping his forehead with his sleeve. His deformity was extreme, affecting his legs as well as his spine but his head was magnificent, a young Socrates. Wycliffe was reminded of those seaside photographs where the victim is persuaded to push his head through a hole thereby lending a face to a grotesque figure. But it's not funny when nature herself plays the joke.

'Good morning.'

Dampier answered with a quick smile.

'My goodness, that was a stiff climb!' Wycliffe said.

'It's quite easy when you do it often and it's good exercise.'

He had a pleasant cultured voice, assured despite a certain shyness of manner. 'Are you a visitor?'

Wycliffe introduced himself and Dampier smiled.

'No need then, for me to tell you who I am.'

'I intended to come and see you, but not at seven-thirty in the morning. I'm out for a pre-breakfast stroll but I'll trouble you a little later in the day if I may.'

He saw Dampier's involuntary glance back at the bungalow.

'No time like the present.'

'Good! You knew Miss Welles, of course?'

'Very well.'

'How long?'

Dampier considered. 'I met her first about seven years ago when she was down on holiday but I have known her well only since she came to Kergwyns to live – about five years, I suppose it must be.'

'When did you last see her?'

'She was at my house on Wednesday evening along with other friends.'

'Mr Lomax?'

Dampier's eyes narrowed. 'Among others, yes.'

'Did she seem to be her usual self?'

'Her usual self,' Dampier repeated the words as though they presented a problem. 'It's difficult to say, she seemed depressed but that was not unusual.'

'Do you know any special reason why she might have been depressed on that occasion?'

A slight shrug of irritation. 'She wasn't by nature a sanguine person.'

'You don't know, for example, that she was pregnant?'

No sign of surprise. Dampier had himself well in hand; a formidable man. 'I didn't know that she was pregnant,' he answered, without expression.

'Does it surprise you?'

He hesitated. 'Yes, I think it does.'

'Can you make any suggestion as to the father of the child?'

'No.'

'Could it possibly have been you?'

Dampier returned the superintendent's stare, unflinching. 'It's possible but extremely unlikely.'

Wycliffe relaxed. 'Thank you, that was very frank.'

It was natural for them to walk back together through the gorse, both of them uneasily conscious of being watched from the window.

'I live in the first bungalow.'

They stopped at the gate. 'You realize that we may have further questions for you or your sister, Mr Dampier, but that is all for the moment.'

Dampier nodded. 'I quite understand.' As he opened the gate a huge tabby cat padded towards him and rubbed round his legs. 'That reminds me, what happened to her cat?'

The superintendent was curt. 'I've no idea.'

He was getting the feel of the place, getting to know the people who knew Pussy Welles and that was something. It might not be the best way to conduct an inquiry but for him it was the only way. He had to think himself, almost live himself, into the world which had been the victim's. Darley would look after the routine with superb efficiency and feel with some justification that he was carrying the brunt of the case, but Darley was made for martyrdom and enjoyed it.

He went into breakfast and was given VIP treatment by Sylvie who seemed to have taken him under her wing.

After breakfast Darley telephoned.

'She was definitely married to that fellow Horner. The marriage took place in a Willesden Register Office only a month before they settled in St Ives. She was married in the name of Welles because her parents both died when she was very young and a couple of that name adopted her. They had a bookshop in Richmond but they're retired now and nobody seems to know where they've gone. The girl worked as a secretary but again, nobody can remember where.'

'You've dropped a word to the press – asked for their co-operation et cetera?'

'Of course!'

Of course! He had only said it because Darley expected him to say something. 'I'm surprised that the press haven't turned up here yet.'

'They will.'

An awkward silence.

'Have you any special instructions, sir?'

'What? No, I don't think so. I expect you'll keep busy.'

'I've got the inquest at eleven.'

'Yes, and, incidentally, let me know the arrangements for the funeral. If a relative doesn't turn up . . .'

He dropped the receiver feeling that he had gone down one step further in Darley's estimation. Then he went out into the square, as peaceful as ever; a postman delivering letters, a white dog sunning himself in the middle of the road and a little boy sitting on the steps of the war memorial reading a comic. An old yellow bus rattled in and pulled up by the church. The driver shut off the engine, got out and lit a cigarette, leaning against the wall of the churchyard. Soon people began to arrive in ones and twos, mostly women with shopping bags but sometimes a couple, the men in dark suits which only saw the light once or twice in a week.

'Where are they going?' Wycliffe strolled over and stood by the little boy.

'Penzance. It's Saturday.' He didn't look up from reading his comic.

Wycliffe thought it would be a good time to call on the Barneses. He continued across the square and followed a winding lane between granite hedges, out on to the road. As he stood at the junction, the yellow bus passed him and chugged off in the direction of Penzance. He watched it snake round the bends until it was out of sight then took the opposite direction. He found the path to the cove, walked past the farm, past the Barnes' car parked in a clearing and on to the cottage. The door was open but there was nobody about so he knocked. A young woman in a quilted dressing gown came down the passage and he recognized her as the girl from the Mini. It was obvious that she recognized him but they were formal.

'Mrs Barnes? – Superintendent Wycliffe. I would like a word with your husband.'

'I'm afraid my husband isn't up yet; perhaps you will call back later.' Firm, distant.

'It's important and I'd rather wait.'

Then a man's voice from upstairs. 'For God's sake let him in, Ursie, and tell him I'll be down in a minute.'

She shrugged. 'In there.'

A little sitting-room, low ceilinged and dimly lit, the window almost blocked by ivy.

'I'm sorry to come at an inconvenient time.'

No answer. When he was seated in an armchair with broken springs, she said, 'My husband will be down shortly,' then she went out, closing the door behind her.

He could imagine the crisis between them, the armed truce that now prevailed. Barnes had probably counted on an impulsive emotional confession demanding quick and loving absolution; penitence in a warm embrace.

'I can't think what came over me! To treat you the way I did . . . I must have been mad!'

And she was supposed to say: 'Don't think of it, darling – you know it doesn't matter between us – not really . . .'

But it had mattered to Ursula. She was profoundly

shocked and she didn't want to talk about it or anything else. All she said was: 'You must give me time to think. I must get used to the idea.'

Now, twenty-four hours had passed and she was still tight lipped and silent. Well, she probably had more shocks coming to her, poor girl.

Wycliffe wished that he had waited outside where he could have smoked his pipe. He felt imprisoned in the dim little room, silent except for the noise of the stream by the gate. They must have taken over the furniture with the cottage; a chiffonier, and Edwardian version of *His* and *Her* chairs, a grotesquely ugly overmantel. Either they had an academic detachment which allowed them to live with it or they were the trend setters in a cult of Edwardiana. He was plucking up courage to go out into the garden when he heard footsteps on the stairs and a moment later Barnes came in, sullenly apologetic. He looked haggard and he was unshaven and unwashed. Wycliffe noticed the weakness of his mouth and chin; a man who might kill from fear but not for jealousy or revenge. He slumped into a chair by the window.

'This is a terrible business.'

'I want to ask you about your association with Miss Welles.'

He nodded. No attempt at evasion.

'When did you last see her?'

The question seemed unexpected and he shifted uneasily in his chair. 'On Wednesday afternoon, the day before she died. I called at the cottage after lunch.'

'You didn't see her again on the Thursday?'

'No.'

Wycliffe sat forward in his chair, causing it to creak alarmingly. He spoke quietly. 'It is fair to tell you, Dr Barnes, that you were seen in the neighbourhood of the cottage after ten o'clock on Thursday night. According to the pathologist the shooting occurred somewhere between nine-thirty and midnight.'

Barnes said nothing.

'You see that your position is serious unless you offer some explanation.'

'I did go to the cottage on Thursday evening but I did not see her.'

'Why not?'

'For the simple reason that she didn't answer the door. I rang but there was no answer.'

'So what did you do?'

'I came away.'

'Were there any lights on in the cottage?'

'Yes, upstairs and down.'

'And yet you came away?'

Barnes seemed embarrassed. 'Yes.'

'Did you hear any music coming from the cottage?'

'Music?'

'The record player.'

'No.'

'Did Miss Welles often fail to answer the door to you?'

'It happened. It meant that it was not a suitable time to call.'

'Perhaps you had a special ring?'

He nodded. 'Yes.'

Wycliffe got up and stood with his back to the fireplace looking down on the seated Barnes. He felt restless, cramped, unable to concentrate in this dark poky little room. 'When you saw her on Wednesday or at any earlier time, did you form the impression that she might be in serious trouble?'

'No.'

'Or danger?'

'Certainly not!'

'Did she ever attempt to blackmail you?'

'How could she?'

'By threatening to tell your wife.'

'No. In any case, she wasn't that sort of girl. She was highly intelligent and sensitive. I can't imagine her trying to blackmail anybody.'

'Did you pay her?'

Barnes made an angry gesture. 'She wasn't a common prostitute!'

Wycliffe frowned. 'I'm not mincing words, Dr Barnes; this is a murder case and you would do well to remember it. This girl was, to say the least, unconventional in her relationships with men and I am asking whether you paid her for her favours to you?'

'It wasn't like that.'

'Then what was it like?'

'From time to time there were small loans.'

'Loans not intended to be repaid, is that it?'

He nodded.

'And what did these loans amount to?'

'A few pounds at a time, not a great deal.'

'Enough to be financially embarrassing?'

A momentary hesitation. 'No.'

Wycliffe's manner became conversational again. 'Were you in love with her?'

'No.'

'Then why did you become involved?'

Barnes looked at him as though the question was an absurdity. 'Surely you understand that some men feel that they are missing something in marriage?'

'And look elsewhere for it?'

'I wasn't actually looking.'

'You mean that it was offered?'

'I suppose you could say that.'

'Are you in love with your wife?'

'Yes!'

As though upon her cue, Ursula Barnes came in; she had changed into a well washed linen dress, pale green and rather too long to be fashionable. She sat down on an upright chair without looking at her husband. 'You don't mind, superintendent?'

'It's up to your husband, Mrs Barnes.'

Barnes shrugged, probably implying that what he thought wouldn't make any difference. Wycliffe continued.

'Did you know that Miss Welles was pregnant?'

'Pregnant?' His surprise seemed genuine. 'I don't believe it!'

'A pathologist doesn't make that kind of mistake, Dr Barnes.'

'Did she know?' He looked nervously at his wife but she seemed indifferent. 'I mean . . .'

'It was eight or nine weeks so she must have had a pretty good idea.' Wycliffe cursed himself for allowing Barnes to sit between him and the light. 'Is it possible that you were the father?'

'No, it is quite impossible.'

'How can you be sure?' The question came not from the superintendent but from his wife. 'After all, Richard, you were involved with her in a way that has been known to have that result.'

Wycliffe was revising his ideas of Ursula. She had not come in to protect her husband but to derive a malevolent satisfaction from his humiliation. Barnes looked at her with a pained expression before replying.

'If you must know, she was fanatically careful.'

It was Wycliffe who wanted to change the subject. 'Where did you first meet her?'

'We met her at a party, about a year ago.'

'At the Dampiers'?'

'Yes.'

Wycliffe reseated himself in the chair with broken springs. 'What were your impressions of the dead girl, Mrs Barnes?'

She swept the hair from her brow with a quick movement. 'I distrusted her from the start; she was the sort of woman who preys upon men.'

'I am being indiscreet, but my questions are necessary. When did you begin to suspect that your husband was having an affair with her?'

The answer was immediate. 'I didn't suspect; I thought he had more . . .' She stopped herself; perhaps she was going to say more sense or more integrity, but whatever it was, she changed her mind. 'I neither knew nor suspected anything until Richard told me about it after she was dead.'

'Why did you tell your wife at all?' Wycliffe turned to Barnes.

'Why? I should have thought that was obvious.'

'Because he thought I would be sure to find out.' Ursula spoke with a sneer. Reconciliation was still a long way off.

The superintendent changed his ground once more. 'Did she ever speak of her past life – of her life before she came to Kergwyns?'

'Never.'

'But you knew that you were not the only man in her life?'

'I knew that there had been others.'

'Had been?'

48

'All right, still were.'

'Dampier for one?'

'Yes, Dampier.'

'That was understandable,' Ursula put in quickly. 'If you have seen John, you must realize that he couldn't . . . that it would have been difficult for him to lead a normal life – to marry and have children. The way he sees it, it would be impossible. Even if he found a woman willing to have him, he couldn't allow himself to impose his misfortune on her, to let her carry his burden . . .'

'But surely, his sister is doing precisely that, and Pussy Welles . . .'

'That is quite different!' Ursula interrupted. 'Erica is devoted to him and as for that girl . . .'

Obviously she was less than a woman; a mere safety valve for the noble repressions of the hunchback. Wycliffe had had enough. He stood up. 'Thank you for your help; I shall probably have to come again but meantime, I will send someone along to take your statement, Dr Barnes.'

'My statement?' Barnes looked surprised.

'Of course, about your visit on Wednesday afternoon and your second visit on Thursday evening.'

Barnes walked with him to the gate. The sky had clouded over and heavy drops of rain threatened a downpour but Wycliffe lingered. Now he was in the open he felt in no hurry. 'Can you suggest anyone who might have feared or hated her enough to kill her?'

'No, I can't. The very idea seems absurd.'

'And yet she is dead.'

Wycliffe knew too well that in a case of murder it is a mistake to search for a dramatic or even an *adequate* motive; most killings are done for reasons that seem trivial to all but the killer and so the victim's death appears mysterious and unaccountable. Barnes shivered; perhaps because he was coatless and the cold raindrops made large damp patches on the material of his shirt, perhaps because his thoughts were harrowing.

'I can't imagine who would want to kill her.'

Wycliffe looked at him thoughtfully and murmured half to himself, 'She was killed by a jealous lover, a jealous wife or a very frightened man.' He turned up the collar of his raincoat and hurried off up the path, leaving Barnes looking after him, worried, puzzled, apprehensive.

By the time he reached the road it was raining in earnest. He could have stayed out the shower at the cottage but he liked to withdraw at what he considered to be the right psychological moment. He had no faith in sustained interrogation, little and often was his recipe. Just keep coming back.

The fact that she was pregnant probably explained why she had been worried, why, according to Lomax, she needed money. It fitted with her 'you owe me nothing but there are those who do'. Presumably Barnes was one. He suspected that Barnes had parted with more money than he would admit. If she had pressed him hard, might he have killed her? A weak character driven to desperation. Then there was Dampier – no weakness there, but deformity. Is it possible for a *normal* mind to cohabit with such gross deformity of body? He had seen Dampier on the cliffs exhausting himself in frenzied purposeless endeavour like Quasimodo on the bells. For the first time it occurred to him to associate the tortured malformation of Dampier's body with the secret blemish on the murdered girl. Had she been so morbidly conscious of her own aberration that she could identify herself with his monstrosity? Was the removal of her shoe and stocking after death to be seen as a declaration? Then there were the women to be remembered – Ursula Barnes, Erica Dampier and how many others?

He had been walking almost oblivious of the rain until he realized that he was wet across the shoulders, that water was dripping down his neck from his sodden cap. The whole moorland seemed like a green-brown sponge oozing rivulets of brown water over the tarmac. At one point where a farm entrance bridged the ditch, a blockage sent a river of fluid mud across the road so that he was forced to wade almost ankle deep. He reached the inn at last and went to his room to change without seeing anyone. A warm appetizing smell spiced with garlic came up from the kitchen which seemed to be beneath his room. He could hear the rattle of pans and crocks and a girl's voice singing. He wondered if Sylvie did the cooking as well as everything else.

When he was standing in his shirt, there was a tap at the door and he put on his dressing gown. It was Sylvie, holding an envelope by one corner.

'What is it?'

'It's for you, it came just after you went out, dropped into the letter box with the rest of the post. I haven't shown it to him.' She was conspiratorial.

A cheap envelope addressed in pencilled capitals. He was familiar enough with these.

'Didn't you ought to test it for fingerprints?'

The message, also in pencilled letters was brief:

BARNES HAS OR HAD AN AUTOMATIC PISTOL

Nothing remarkable under the circumstances about an anonymous letter. Every murder case brought a crop of them, some malicious, most of them crazy, the odd one now and then, informative. But they all had to be investigated. He had to admit that few were as explicit as this one and if Barnes did possess an automatic and if it turned out to have been recently fired and if . . . Well, put all the ifs together and there might be the beginnings of a case.

Chapter Three

At the start of his affair with Pussy Welles, Richard
Barnes could look back upon four blameless years of
marriage to Ursula. On the whole, they had been
four good years, they got on well together. Ursula
liked to manage people and Richard had no objection
to being managed, they were both involved in interesting academic work and neither of them wanted children.
It seemed a pretty good recipe for marriage and it
worked. But as time went on Richard began to be
troubled by vague dissatisfactions, he felt that in the
even tenor of their ways, in their tacit acceptance of
each other, in the very stability of their relationship,
they were missing something. At least, he was. And he
was not long in reaching a conclusion about the source
of his discontent. There was no adventure and little
romance left in their marriage. He blamed Ursula for
this; she had domesticated sex. Before their marriage,
she had been very thoroughly into the subject of marital
love through the media of both literature and expert
consultation and even after they were married she
continued to study their relationship as though it was
a subject for a projected thesis. In short, and in
Richard's opinion, she had acquired an objective and
clinical approach which came near to sterilizing their
embraces. He could still derive the keenest anticipatory
pleasure from her petite blonde body but in its climax,

their lovemaking seemed to be at the level of hygienic eroticism.

It is probable that like thousands of other couples they would have gone on making the best of this rather poor bargain if Ursula had not come into money. From the modest competence of their combined university salaries they entered upon relative affluence. And the first thing they did was to buy a cottage in a charming valley near the village of Kergwyns on the north Cornish coast. It was during their first vacation in the cottage that they met Pussy Welles and it was during that same vacation that Richard made her his mistress. At least that was how he saw it.

Richard, like most men, thought of himself as having a way with women, though he would have had difficulty in finding justification for thinking anything of the kind. But it was confidence born of this unwarranted assumption which encouraged him to enter so lightheartedly into his relationship with Pussy Welles. It was all so delightfully simple and it solved his problem. True, there had to be a little deception, but as life with Ursula seemed to benefit rather than otherwise, he was not troubled in his conscience for long. By the end of the Easter vacation he felt that he had discovered the secret of the good life. There was nothing sordid about it, their assignations were occasions for gaiety and mirth and they achieved undreamed of satisfaction in each other's arms. From time to time, quite suddenly and inconsequentially, Pussy would say, 'Oh, Richard! – lend me a few quid, I have to pay the milk bill.' So that he was never in a position of having to actually pay her; she was far too civilized and sophisticated for that.

During the following summer and Christmas vacations their liaison continued and flourished. The sums which Pussy 'borrowed' increased, causing Richard some misgivings. 'I wonder if you could manage a fiver to tide me over until Saturday, Ricky, darling . . .' Luckily, and surprisingly, Ursula had become quite casual about money so that a few pounds here or there hardly seemed to matter. And it was well worth it. He was a new man; his work prospered, his outlook grew more mature, more tolerant, and he felt affectionately protective towards Ursula. Such benefits accrue when the sacred and the profane are kept decently apart.

His main difficulty had been to explain his absences to Ursula but he soon acquired an astonishing facility at contriving situations in which it seemed natural for them to be apart so that he was able to achieve three and sometimes four meetings a week while they were at the cottage.

The crisis came during their second Easter at Kergwyns. Ursula was a moderator for some intermediate examinations and she had to remain up during the first week of the vacation. The opportunity was heaven sent, but he must be discreet.

'I don't want to go down without you, darling.'

'Don't be silly, Richard. You'll have a week of peace and quiet to spend on your book.'

'Well, there is that . . . if you don't mind . . .'

'Silly boy!'

He wrote to Pussy Welles at once telling her the good news.

And so, early on a fine Monday morning, he stacked the car with clean linen and provisions and set out. By midday he was approaching St Ives with the great panoramic sweep of the bay on his right; the blue-green sea shattering the sunlight into a million dazzling fragments; the lighthouse on its little island, whiter than white. Too good to be true – a story book picture – *First Day of the Holiday*. Five minutes edging through the narrow streets of the town, a long climb, and he was out on the moor in sight of the sea again. The gorse was more golden than he had ever known, the dead stalks of last year's bracken made great splashes of rusty red, and the grey-green lichens softened the giant granite outcrops so that they looked tamed, amenable.

A mile along the road, within sight of the square squat tower of Kergwyns church, he turned off down a rutted track in the direction of the sea. Past the entrance to a farm the track petered out in a clearing almost enclosed by blackthorn and goat willow. He left the car there and followed a footpath for fifty yards, over the dark waters of a little stream to a second clearing where the cottage was, hemmed in on three sides by a coppice of sycamores. The stream and the footpath continued together past the gate of the cottage towards the cove, half a mile down the valley. Apart from the noise of the stream it was a silent place, still; even in the sunshine the light was mellow. To some it might seem sinister but Richard loved it; he looked forward especially to these first moments of arrival and savoured them as a connoisseur of sensual pleasure. The little garden was choked with ferns and the cobbled path carpeted in moss; the air was moist and laden with the blended indefinable scents of thrusting growth and equally vigorous decay.

He removed the white card from the front door: *Ursula and Richard Barnes. Redirected mail to . . .* and their address. They never locked the door, which was foolish, but it was another way of emphasizing that this was their special place, that it was different. First he would light the fire to air the place, then he would unpack the car . . . His eyes rested on the telephone – their only amenity – Ursula called it. Should he ring now? Or save it until he had done the chores? He was like an adolescent, unsure of the reception he would get from his first love, eager to put it to the test. He picked up the receiver and dialled her number. The tantalizing wait, punctuated by those absurd noises that mock at our most profound emotions. He willed her to be there and to answer. She was in the kitchen preparing her midday meal; the muffled ringing came through from the little hall at the front of the house. She was wearing her blue flowered housecoat, her auburn hair caught with a slide at the back, like a little girl's. She never hurried. He imagined her drying her hands, walking calmly, gracefully, through the sitting-room, opening the little white door with the glass panels, reaching for the receiver . . . he waited for the click . . . but it never came. He waited through an interminable number of rings before deciding that she was out. He was just replacing the receiver when he heard her voice, musical, controlled, 'Kergwyns 42'.

'It's me – Ricky.'

'Oh, so you're down already.'

'I told you in my letter. Ursula has to stay up for another week, so I'm alone . . . Can I see you?'

'When?'

'Tonight at the cottage?'

'Why at the cottage?'

'I told you I'm alone, and you remember the last time?' He tried to breathe warmth and tenderness into the telephone.

'All right, then.'

'What time?'

Hesitation. 'I'll come when I can.' She dropped the telephone.

Her coldness rebuffed him, but it would be different when she came. He set about his tasks, trying to shake off a lingering sense of anti-climax. After lunch out of tins he walked down to the cove killing time. Early in their acquaintanceship, Pussy had warned him in her bantering way.

'All you want from me is the one thing your wife doesn't give you; ours is a convenient arrangement, an accommodation. It's not romance.'

She was right, of course. He tried to reconcile himself to the knowledge that she had other men. Why should it matter? But it did.

From six o'clock, he was on tenterhooks. Would she come for a meal? Once, when Ursula had gone away overnight she came to the cottage and they cooked omelettes on the bottle gas cooker and ate them in front of the fire, drinking a whole bottle of wine between them. She had stayed the night, the only time in his life when he had actually slept with another woman. Well, he had plenty of eggs and cheese and tomatoes and wine, and he had aired the bed. He sat in the living-room with the wireless playing softly, watching the window, watching the light turn yellow, then fade almost to darkness before she came.

'I couldn't come before.'

He took her coat and she stood in the firelight. She looked chaste in her white blouse and black skirt, just standing there, but when she walked, the sway of her hips and the way she held herself so that her breasts protruded . . . He took her in his arms but she disengaged herself.

'Later, Ricky!' She chided him like a fond mother,

her voice reproving, but full of promise. She kissed his cheek. The old magic.

'Will you have something to eat?'

'No thanks, I've had a meal.'

'Drink?'

'All right, make it a gin if you've got some.'

He handed her the drink and sat opposite her, feasting his eyes. It seemed incredible that directly she would allow him to possess her. She was the kind of girl that every man would stop to look at as she passed down the street; the very antithesis of Ursula. Not but what Ursula had a lovely body, but clothed in her habitual woolly jumper and tweed skirt, she looked dumpy, homely. Pussy's skirt clung to her – like fur.

The little bedroom was warmed by the flue from the fire below. The double bed and a dressing-table filled almost all the space and the soft light from an oil lamp, suspended, glowed on the motley colours of Ursula's patchwork quilt.

He watched her undress, slowly, deliberately, grace-fully. It occurred to him that she was a professional doing her job in a thoroughly professional way, study-ing the needs of a client and meeting them. He banished the thought as unworthy. He preferred to believe that she enjoyed making love; certainly if she had been entirely mercenary, she could have done a great deal better for herself. He could never make up his mind about Pussy.

Making love with her was like playing an intricate game which you know you are going to win in the end. She had the art of turning each encounter into an opportunity for fresh conquest, seeming to resist each phase in the progress of love until overcome by blandishment; defeated by the consummate skill of her lover, she could resist no longer. In another age and another place, she might have been one of the great courtesans.

She stayed the night. When Richard woke in the morning he was momentarily shocked by the auburn head on his wife's pillow, then he remembered and reached out a hand to stroke her body. She turned over on to her back, wide awake at once, like someone who sleeps on guard. She sat up, pushing her hair back with a sweeping movement of both hands. Outside everything was grey and raindrops chased each other down the little window panes.

'Damn! It's raining.'

'It doesn't matter, I'll run you back in the car.'

'You can drop me at the corner, I don't want to give them more to gossip about than they've got already.'

She lit a cigarette; he fondled her bare breast without achieving the slightest response.

'Ricky . . .'

He raised himself on his elbow. 'What is it?'

She studied the glowing end of her cigarette. 'I need some money.'

'Well?'

'A lot of money.'

'How much?'

She exhaled the blue smoke slowly, watching it rise in a thin spiral column to the ceiling. 'A hundred and fifty pounds, and I need it quickly – before the week is out.'

'But . . .' He was scared, but before he could say more she stopped him.

'Before you start to argue, Ricky, listen!' Her voice was hard, her features cast in a mould that he scarcely recognized. 'You've had what you wanted from me at less than the price of a street girl. What I'm asking for is just something off the arrears; something on account.'

She got out of bed and began to collect her clothes. With complete irrelevance he realized for the first time that she dyed her hair. She was fair – like Ursula! Why hadn't he seen that before? Certainly not for the want of opportunity. She was a cheat! Absurdly, irrationally, this distressed him as much as her demand for money.

'But I don't think I can get hold of a hundred and fifty pounds without Ursula knowing . . .'

'That's your problem!' She sat on the foot of the bed, brushing her hair.

He was silent, calculating. He might just manage it. 'Well?'

'I'll see what I can do.'

'Good! You mustn't run up debts you can't pay.'

With that, she reverted to normal. They had breakfast together, she chatted away, giving him the latest news, and when he dropped her at the corner where the road to the village left the main road, she said:

'Shall I see you tonight?'

He stopped himself from saying 'Yes', just in time. 'No, not tonight, I must get in some work on my book.'

He turned the car and drove back over the shining wet road muttering to himself in time with the sweep of the screen wipers. 'Bloody fool! Bloody fool! Bloody, bloody, bloody, fool.' He parked the car in the clearing and returned to the cottage. He would have liked to tell Ursula the whole story, to throw himself on her mercy, but he dared not.

'It isn't that I'm narrow minded. Rationally, I know that a man sleeping with another woman may mean almost nothing, but in practice, I don't know . . . If you ever did it, Richard, I think I should feel that I had failed you – let you down. I should lose confidence in myself – I don't think I could carry on. I really don't.' That had been Ursula's reaction to the misconduct of one of Richard's colleagues.

'I mean, a successful marriage is so much a matter of mutual trust . . . No, I just couldn't face it.'

They ran a joint bank account but since his association with Pussy Welles, he had opened a secret account, paying in small sums whenever he could to provide for his vacation expenses. He thought that there was something over a hundred pounds in his account and he could draw that out with, perhaps, twenty from their joint account; that would be as much as he dared and it would have to do. He went back to the car and drove to St Ives, to the bank, coming away with a hundred and thirty-six pounds in notes – the price of folly. Suddenly the whole affair had become squalid, it had turned sour on him. Why? Was it because he was being asked to pay the market price for what he wanted instead of getting it on the cheap? However he thought of it he could find no shred of comfort, no salve for his injured pride. My God! – but he would know better in the future! And then he thought of Ursula with shame and humility and warm affection – he would make it up to her.

Next morning – Wednesday – he had heard nothing further from Pussy Welles and they had made no arrangement for him to hand over the money. He wanted to be clear of it, to close the episode; and Ursula would be arriving on Friday. He decided to lunch at the inn, to fortify himself with a few drinks and to go along to Pussy's house afterwards. He walked to Kergwyns in the watery April sunshine. The square was empty and silent, the grey granite and the grey-blue slate made it seem grim, almost sinister. The church-yard boasted a little coppice of wind stunted sycamores, now in pale green leaf, otherwise only the lichens provided any splash of colour.

The bar was empty except for the landlord, reading his newspaper spread on the counter.

'Morning, Dr Barnes. I heard you were with us again.'

'Morning, Mike.'

'The usual?'

Richard's usual was a light ale. He would have liked a short drink but he was flattered at having his taste remembered.

'Have one with me, Mike.'

He was of a timid disposition and he felt gratified to be on easy terms with a great brute of a man like the landlord.

'Mrs Barnes not with you?'

He entered into a more detailed explanation than was necessary and stopped himself too late when he saw Young looking at him, an amused, slightly contemptuous smile on the expressive half of his face. He changed the subject hastily. 'I suppose you can fix me up with lunch, Mike?'

Young turned over the page of his newspaper. 'I suppose I shall have to, Dr Barnes, it wouldn't do if we bachelors didn't stick together, would it?'

After lunch he went along to the cottage resolved to be distant, matter-of-fact and to make an unequivocal break, but his antagonism had evaporated. He was prepared to admit that he owed her more than an occasional pound or two changing hands under the euphemism of a loan. When she answered the door she looked preoccupied and tired but she seemed pleased to see him. She had been working in the sitting-room and there were reference books scattered on the floor and a clip-board of crossword blanks on the arm of her chair.

'I'm trying to make my deadline.'

He said that he didn't want to interrupt but she brushed this aside.

'I'm glad of the excuse.'

Richard was an earnest young man, not to say a little dull, and making up crosswords was an employment unworthy of academic talent. 'I can't understand why you don't do something really creative, Pussy. With your brains and imagination you could *write*.'

She laughed. 'I like doing it and they pay me.'

'But it's only a sort of game.'

'Of course, but what's wrong with that?'

'You could do something *worthwhile*!'

She was teasing him as she often did. 'It depends on what you believe to be worthwhile.'

He stopped to think, trying to say something challenging. 'If you had Aladdin's lamp, what would you do?'

She frowned and pursed her lips. 'I think I'd put myself at the head of a great financial empire – the tycoon of all tycoons.'

'For the money?'

She shook her head. 'No, I don't think the money would interest me. I should do it for the satisfaction in making decisions and watching their repercussions. I should plan and predict then sit back and watch.'

'But you'd have to have some purpose in mind – an aim.'

She looked at him suddenly serious. 'Why? You

throw a stone into a pond just because you want to watch the ripples. That's reason enough.'

'But if it's power you want, why not be a general or a field marshal?'

'All right! I'll settle for a field marshal's baton – but only in wartime; peacetime soldiers are pathetic; children playing with rather stupid toys.'

He was uncomfortable, unable to gauge her mood. 'I hope you'll stick to crosswords.'

'Why?'

'Because people who want power for its own sake are dangerous.'

She was lying back in her chair, relaxed – *available*. He knew that with very little persuasion he could take her upstairs and resume where they had left off. He was tempted but he recalled his panic over the money. It couldn't happen again without Ursula knowing. Suddenly he realized that she was laughing at him.

'You are a timid soul, Richard! Don't you ever feel that you want to live dangerously?'

He was angry. 'No, I don't!'

She looked at him, thoughtful and detached. 'But it isn't your choice is it? Decision is the privilege of the strong.'

He took the envelope containing the money from his pocket and dropped it on the table. 'There's a hundred and thirty-six pounds there. It was all I could manage.'

She glanced at the envelope but said nothing.

'Will it be enough?'

'For what?'

He gestured angrily. 'I think I had better go.'

She did nothing to stop him but she followed him to the door and stood on the step while he covered the little distance to the gate. 'Goodbye, Richard.'

He did not answer. In the lane he met Lomax who looked at him queerly. He had rarely been so angry, never so humiliated.

Ursula was arriving on Friday morning – less than forty-eight hours to go. In that time he must try to close a chapter in his life, banish this girl from his mind, forget the humiliation he had suffered. He was accomplished in the art of forgetting but it took time, and he was anxious that Ursula, quick to sense any sudden change in him, should not probe with solicitous questions. The recipe was exercise and hard work and he followed it conscientiously. His book, a psychological novel, long projected, painfully begun and intermittently pursued, had never received such concentrated attention, and on the Thursday afternoon he walked by the cliff path to St Ives, returning on foot by the road. He was tired but relaxed. He had certainly not forgotten but his recollection was already blurred at the edges, he was in the mood to write it off to experience. Soon his memory would be so hazy that it would be easy to accept a more flattering view of the facts.

He felt hungry and took trouble over preparing his meal, he opened a bottle of wine, found a detective novel which he hadn't read, and settled down to eat. Afterwards he cleared away and washed up ready for Ursula's arrival in the morning. He looked forward to it with warm and tender anticipation. Good old Ursie! Read until bedtime.

Chapter Four

Wycliffe sat back in his chair and placed the palms of his hands together as though in prayer. 'That clears up the details of your visit to the cottage on Wednesday afternoon, Dr Barnes. Now we come to Thursday evening. In your original statement you said that you were not admitted, that you rang the bell and although the house was lit up, no-one answered your ring. This was not unprecedented so after a little wait you returned home. That is what you said – is it in fact what happened? Or do you wish to revise this part of your statement also?'

'No! I mean that it is not exactly what happened and I do want to revise it.'

He looked exhausted and ill, the colour drained from his cheeks, his whole body sagging in the chair. He was demoralized – not because he had been harshly treated – Wycliffe seemed to go out of his way to be courteous, almost respectful in the manner of his questions but he could not disguise their implication. For the first time in his life he had been caught out in a pattern of clumsy lies. Never since he was a schoolboy facing his head-master had he been so called to account. 'But that was not what you said, Dr Barnes . . .' It was devastating: a demeaning experience.

How long had he been there? He had no idea. It seemed that he had spent a significant part of his life slumped in that chair, staring at the window behind the superintendent. The glass had been obscured with white paint which had flaked off, giving a mosaic view of a red brick wall. The light was yellowing so it must be evening. They had given him some tea but he had lunched at home with Ursula. Incredible!

A man has been at St Ives Police Station since two o'clock this afternoon, helping the police with their inquiries . . .

That is what they would be saying on the *News* and in the evening papers. People round their television sets and in pubs would feel just a little more cosy and secure. 'So they got him!'

It had started with the pistol.

After the superintendent's visit and after his statement had been taken, it seemed that with luck the worst might be over. He set about reassuring Ursula, winning her back, and he seemed to be making progress. Oddly, it was by telling her in detail of his affair with Pussy that he began to gain her sympathy and even her understanding. 'You poor simpleton, Richard! Really, you need someone to look after you! But the police can't seriously suspect you of having killed her, can they?'

'Of course not!'

But he didn't tell her of the hundred and thirty-six pounds he had paid to Pussy, nor did he mention the gun. That was left to Superintendent Wycliffe.

It was the Sunday following the murder; they had just finished lunch and Ursula was making coffee while Richard sat at the table, reading. Ursula answered the superintendent's knock.

'I hope I'm not spoiling your lunch, Mrs Barnes. I'll

try not to be too long.' He did not wait to be invited but followed her into the living-room. 'Ah, Dr Barnes – just one or two more questions.'

Richard sat immobile, waiting.

'I understand that you were once a member of an archaeological expedition to the Middle East?'

'Yes, about five or six years ago.'

'You were issued with a .32 automatic pistol?'

'Yes.'

'You did not hand it in at the end of the expedition?'

'No, it was an oversight. Nobody asked for it and I forgot about it until months later.'

'Where is it now?'

'Until recently it was where it has always been with my field gear in a box upstairs.'

'And now?'

He passed a hand over his brow, a hackneyed gesture of despair. 'I don't know; it's gone.'

'Richard!'

'It's true. After I knew that Pussy Welles had been shot, I thought of the gun and I went to look for it – you know how it is – just in case . . .' He seemed to be appealing to the superintendent for understanding but Wycliffe was inscrutable.

'After keeping the gun illegally for a number of years you didn't report its loss?'

'No, I was scared.'

'Is this your gun?' Wycliffe produced a pistol from his pocket. 'We can check, of course, but it will take time.'

Richard took the gun and examined it. 'Yes, I think it's mine – in fact, I'm sure.'

Wycliffe nodded. 'It is also, according to the experts, the gun that killed Miss Welles.'

'But that doesn't mean . . .' Ursula began, then stopped.

'It means that she was shot with a gun for which your husband was responsible. I think you should make a further statement, Dr Barnes – at the station.'

'All right, I will drive over this afternoon.'

'I have a car and driver waiting on the road, Dr Barnes. I think we should get it over.'

But it wasn't over yet; only beginning. They were just getting to the most difficult part.

'After leaving Miss Welles on bad terms on Wednesday afternoon, why did you go to see her again on Thursday evening?'

'She telephoned me at about a quarter to ten saying that she must see me. If I didn't come, I should regret it.'

'She threatened you?'

'I suppose that's what it amounted to but at the time it seemed that she was more distressed than threatening. I didn't want to become involved again but I felt that I must find out what was happening. Pussy wasn't the sort to flap but when I tried to question her on the telephone, she just rang off.'

'So you took your car and drove to Kergwyns. What happened?'

Barnes made a little gesture of revulsion and when he spoke his voice was barely audible so that Wycliffe had to lean forward to catch his words. 'When I arrived, the cottage was lit up as I said and there was no answer to my ring. In the ordinary way, I would have gone back home but in view of her telephone call I had to see her. I banged on the door and it pushed open – it was unfastened – so I went in.' He stopped as though the scene presented itself afresh to his eyes. 'She was lying on the floor – dead.'

Wycliffe waited for him to continue, thinking it best that he should tell his own story, but the silence lengthened and at last, he prompted, 'What did you do?'

'Do? I just stood and looked at her; I was too shocked to do anything.' He spoke like a man drugged, every sentence seemed to cost him a disproportionate effort of thought and enunciation.

'Did you notice anything odd about her?'

'Odd? Yes, she had on only one shoe and stocking and her bare foot was deformed. That somehow made it worse.' A glimmer of animation brought life to his eyes. 'I know it sounds ridiculous but it shocked me almost as much as seeing her dead.'

Wycliffe frowned. 'But you must have known that she had a deformed foot.'

'You would think so, but I didn't. She always wore ankle socks, even when . . . even when she was going to bed. I had never seen her feet uncovered, she used to say that she suffered from bad circulation.' He seemed to dwell on these thoughts and Wycliffe was about to bring him back with a question when he carried on of his own accord. 'I was going to telephone the police – I even went to the porch where the telephone is, then it struck me that Pussy's death would bring everything out into the open. I wanted to avoid that if I could; it would do her no good and it might finish me with my wife . . .'

'What about the gun?'

For the most part Barnes had avoided the super-intendent's eyes, now he looked straight at him. 'I don't know what you mean.'

Wycliffe betrayed the first sign of impatience. 'Dr

Barnes, it must be clear to you that if someone stole your gun for the killing, he would have no reason to remove it from the scene of the crime. If he did, it would be a dangerous embarrassment.' He paused to allow his reasoning to sink in. 'But if you recognized the gun, lying beside the body, it would be quite natural, though unwise, for you to take it and hide it.'

Barnes would have interrupted but Wycliffe wouldn't let him.

'Let me finish! Your gun was found, quite by chance. A culvert beneath a farm entrance between your cottage and the village was blocked so that the drainage water flooded the road. In clearing the culvert, your gun was found, otherwise it might have stayed there for years.' Wycliffe leaned forward and spoke with great earnestness. 'Now, Dr Barnes, let me advise you to be absolutely frank, did you remove that gun and hide it?'

'No, I saw no gun.'

Wycliffe nodded but it was impossible to judge whether he accepted the denial as truth. 'Very well then, what *did* you do?'

It seemed to take a little while for Barnes to re-orientate his thoughts. 'I went upstairs to the bureau to see if she had kept any of my letters or anything else that might involve me, but somebody had got there first; there were no letters or anything of that sort and I found nothing.'

'Nothing, Dr Barnes?' The superintendent waited, then added, 'Remember you are making a fresh statement.'

He seemed to debate within himself and Wycliffe made no attempt to hurry him. At last, he had reached a decision. 'All right! I found the hundred pounds in ten pound notes – still in the paper band as I had it from the bank.'

'And you took it?'

He nodded. 'Not that I wanted the money back but I thought that the bank were bound to have the numbers and that the police would try to trace the money.'

'You still have those notes?'

'No.' He looked sheepish. 'I stopped the car on my way back and stuffed them down a hole in the hedge.'

'A hole in the hedge.' The superintendent's voice was expressionless. 'You could find the place again?'

'I think so.'

'So that having looked for anything that might involve you and having taken the money, you walked out.'

'Yes. I must admit that I was scared.'

There could be no doubt that he had been scared or that he still was. Could his foolish, incriminating behaviour be attributed wholly to that? Or had he been so frightened that as weak men sometimes will he had resorted to a desperate remedy?

Wycliffe asked many more questions. Who visited the cottage regularly? Who else might have known about the gun? Had he ever seen any evidence of intruders? But nothing fresh emerged. The light in the dingy little room faded and the lamp was switched on. Barnes made a new formal statement and signed it. Gradually it was being borne in upon him that he really was under suspicion of murder. Perhaps the superintendent was convinced of his guilt and believed that it was only a matter of time before he admitted it.

'What time is it?'

'Nine o'clock.'

In connection with the Cornish murder a man has been at the St Ives Police Station for seven hours, assisting the police with their inquiries . . . That was what they would be saying on the *News*. And the gossips would say: 'They must be sure of their ground to keep him there like that.'

For long periods of time they seemed to ignore him. People came and went as though he was just part of the furniture but they never left him alone, there was always somebody in the room. If they were going to detain him all night, would they have to charge him? He wouldn't ask questions of that sort – not let them see that he had even considered the possibility. What would happen if he said, 'I am going home. If you want me again, you know where to find me!'? He was deliberating whether to try it when the superintendent came back again after a lengthy absence.

'Well, Dr Barnes, that is all for the moment. Your wife is outside with your car, waiting to take you home.'

For an instant he felt like an animal whose cage is suddenly thrown open, incredulous, suspicious. 'I can go?'

Wycliffe looked at him gravely. 'I have insufficient evidence to detain you, Dr Barnes.'

The man who has been at St Ives Police Station for over eight hours, assisting the police with their inquiries into the Cornish murder, left at a little after ten o'clock this evening. In a brief statement to the press, Super-intendent Charles Wycliffe said that he did not envisage an early arrest.

A set-back for the listeners and watchers.

But the evidence that was to turn the scale came next day, the day of the funeral.

All Darley's efforts had failed to produce a relative. Her mother, by adoption, was dead and her father in a home for the confused elderly. To Wycliffe's surprise, it was Lomax who sought and obtained the coroner's authority to make arrangements for the funeral. And so she was buried in the little churchyard among the slate headstones, an interloper in a company of Nances, Pascoes, Kessells and Trewins.

In a thin grey drizzle a little group of men in raincoats stood round the grave while the vicar read the shortened service. Wycliffe was there, intrigued by his fellow mourners. No women. He was surprised to see Barnes; perhaps his wife thought it impolitic for him to stay away. The innkeeper was there, lugubrious and solemn; Harvey Clemens and Aubrey Reed shared an enormous umbrella and Dampier braved the public gaze for once. Lomax was chief mourner and he was accompanied by a tall, fleshy young man whom Wycliffe identified afterwards as the school teacher, Mitford.

The strangest group of mourners in the superintendent's wide experience. Despite the rain a little knot of villagers waited by the churchyard gate. He could imagine their gossip and scolded himself for seeing a certain humour in the situation.

Mainly because he did not want to walk back with the others, he lingered by the graveside while they trooped to the gate under an archway of dripping sycamores. Then he saw a woman in a plum coloured raincoat, with an umbrella to match, picking her way among the graves towards him, her absurd little high heels clutching at the spongy ground with every step.

'Superintendent Wycliffe? Elsa Cooper.'

She was younger than he had supposed, now that he could see her face, not much over thirty, a plump, self contained woman, her features a little coarse and hard.

She obviously managed something, a small hotel, a hairdresser's, a dress shop – perhaps a café. She had that indefinable air of experience which Wycliffe had known so well among a certain class of women in the city. Not easily frightened. 'I wanted to speak to you. I was a friend of Pussy Welles.'

A woman friend!

Wycliffe was wet already and getting wetter. The woman's umbrella was merely an irritation, a threat at the level of his eyes. 'Let's find somewhere dry.' And they moved into the shelter of the church porch and sat side by side on the wormeaten bench like lovers escaping from the rain.

It turned out that she owned a boarding house in St Ives.

'I got to know Pussy when she came to St Ives on holiday; she stayed at my place there years running, though it wasn't mine then, mother was still alive.'

'Did she come alone or with her family?'

'Oh, she was alone. She was a typist or secretary or something in London and she wasn't short of money.'

'She would have been about nineteen or twenty, I suppose, when you first knew her?'

'About that. She was four years younger than me. Anyway, when she got married and they came to St Ives to live, we stayed friendly – not what you might call close, but she would occasionally drop in of a morning for coffee and we would have a shopping spree now and then in Penzance. After Arthur, that was her husband, was killed, we kept in touch; she moved out here and whenever I felt like a gossip I would ring her up and she would do the same. That's what happened on Thursday evening.'

'Thursday evening?'

'The night she was killed.'

'You rang her up?'

'No, she rang me.' She stood up, divesting herself of her raincoat, and began to shake it vigorously. 'This damned rain! There's no end to it! She wanted my advice.'

She seemed to expect the superintendent to ask the obvious question but as he remained silent she went on: 'Pussy was pregnant and she wanted to know if I would help her.'

'In what way?'

She gave him a look of contempt. 'What sort of help does an unmarried girl need when she's pregnant? Do I have to spell it out?'

Wycliffe was unperturbed. 'Are you an abortionist, then?'

'No, I'm not! And if that's all the thanks I get for coming to you, I can go again.' The superintendent said nothing but she made no attempt to go. 'I am not an abortionist but neither am I wet behind the ears. I've been around and I might have helped Pussy if this hadn't happened. You see, I'm being frank.'

'The world is hard on us women and we've got to stick together,' Wycliffe said tonelessly.

Her anger flared in a look. 'You know all the answers, don't you?'

'I've heard them so many times before. Never mind, what happened on the telephone?'

She shrugged. 'If it wasn't for the thought of him getting away with it, I wouldn't bother, I'm damned if I would!'

'Who, getting away with it?'

'Dr bloody Barnes. He was with her when she phoned me.'

77

'How do you know?'

'She told me. I asked her if she knew who the father was and she said that she did. Ricky Barnes. Then she said, "He's here now, I'm trying to work out the details with him." I said I hoped the details included some cash and she laughed and said that I needn't worry.'

'What time was this?'

'About a quarter to ten. I was watching a programme on the telly which finished at a quarter to ten and when I came back from talking to her it was over.'

'You are prepared to make a statement?'

'I shouldn't have come if I wasn't.' She fiddled with the clasp of her handbag and seemed ill at ease. 'There's something else.'

'Something else?'

'Pussy was laughing as I told you, then she suddenly got serious. She spoke almost in a whisper so that I could hardly hear her. "If anything happens to me, Elsa," she said, "remember I told you." I asked her what she meant but she wouldn't say any more. When I pressed her she said to forget it, that she was only joking. You could never tell with Pussy.'

'Did you take her seriously?'

'Not at the time – not really.'

'But you do now?'

'What do you think?'

Wycliffe regarded her gravely. 'This happened last Thursday evening and you must have heard on Friday that she was dead, now it's Monday. You haven't hurried yourself.'

She stood up and began to put on her raincoat. 'I've had dealings with the police before and the local bunch don't have a very high opinion of me. I might easily have got short changed. Then I thought of coming to see you. Anyway, you can make what you like of it, I've got to get back.'

'Wait! You knew Pussy Welles three years before she came to live here, did she know anyone else in the district at that time?'

She gave him a knowing look. 'You mean any of the Kergwyns lot? She got herself mixed up with Mike Young, he was quite the lad about town in those days, believe it or not. She used to go out to Kergwyns so I suppose she must have come across the others but she never mentioned them to me that I can remember.'

'Did she ever speak to you of her home or her people?'

'I don't think so; not much anyway. I remember her father kept a shop of some sort in Richmond and she worked in the City I think, but that's about all.'

'No talk of boy friends?'

'Not really. I remember her telling me once that there was a man who had taken a fancy to her, giving her expensive presents, that sort of thing. I had the impression he was her boss but I may be wrong. Anyway he must have been a lot older than her for she spoke of him as "my old man".'

'It couldn't have been Arthur Horner?'

She shook her head decisively. 'No. That was a whirlwind courtship and marriage; in any case he was very little older than her.'

'One more question: you say you were her friend, what did you think of her?'

She seemed surprised by the question and looked at him doubtfully before answering. 'Think of her? – I suppose I thought she was a queer sort of girl. Not my sort really; for one thing she was well educated and I think she came from a good home, but she had to have men.' She paused, screwed up her snub little nose. 'I've never understood her. She didn't do it for the money, that's certain; she could have made a living easily enough without that. And yet she hated the men she went with.'

'Hated them?'

'That's what I said. At least, she despised them. Not at first, of course, when they were new, but it wasn't long before she would change. The funny thing was, she was reluctant to give them up . . . as I said I never understood her. There was something strange about her attitude to men – something a bit frightening.'

'Frightening?' Wycliffe tried to get her to enlarge on the word but she couldn't or wouldn't. He watched her tapping her way down the path to the gate and sat for some time before getting up to follow.

Well, he had more than enough evidence for an arrest. Not from the best sources but it was enough to force his hand. He walked slowly back through the rain to the inn where Inspector Darley was waiting for him. He took no satisfaction in the prospect of this arrest. It was not the logical outcome of a process of patient investigation and study, of fact and reason; it was a course forced upon him by an accumulation of damning evidence which he had not even sought. He did not necessarily believe that Barnes was innocent, equally, he was unconvinced of his guilt, but there is a point beyond which a police officer must act on the evidence whatever he thinks of it. Darley could not understand him.

'The court will decide whether he's guilty; it's not our problem.'

This trite statement of the obvious did nothing to improve the superintendent's temper.

They were sitting in a little private room at the inn which the landlord had offered for their use. There were wicker chairs and small circular tables with beer mats and little else.

'All right, let's hear the case as we shall put it to the DPP.'

Darley rubbed his chin and prepared to expound. 'In the first place, Barnes was having an affair with the deceased. On his own admission, she had been making increasing demands for money and the day before her death, he claims to have paid her more than a hundred and thirty pounds – the sort of sum he couldn't raise twice without his wife's knowledge.' Darley had produced his notebook and was leafing through the pages, his great index finger followed the lines of a paragraph here and there.

'We know that the girl was pregnant and, according to this Cooper woman, she believed that Barnes was the child's father. Cooper also says that she was trying to secure an abortion and, presumably, it was for that she needed the money.'

'But he had already paid her the money,' Wycliffe intervened. 'There is nothing to suggest that she was asking for more.'

Darley smiled. 'I've thought of that. Barnes certainly drew a hundred and thirty-six pounds from the bank but we only have his word for it that he paid it over. All we found of the money was thirty odd pounds. I know he claims to have taken back the tenners and hidden them to protect himself but that money hasn't been found and he seems unable to help.'

Wycliffe sighed. 'I don't know where that gets us, but go on, anyway.'

Darley heaved his great bulk forward in his chair to

get a better light on his notebook. 'Then, of course, there's the pistol. He used a weapon which he had had by him for years and which no-one was supposed to know about; afterwards, he hid it. Should we have found out about the pistol if somebody hadn't written an anonymous note? Finally he is seen on the doorstep of the girl's cottage at ten o'clock. He says that he had just arrived but, according to Elsa Cooper, he was at the cottage when Pussy Welles rang her at a little before quarter to ten.'

Wycliffe stood up and walked to the window. It looked out on a yard stacked with barrels, blocking the light; a high wall shut off the yard from what must be the open land to the cliffs. 'Barnes insists that he wasn't there, that he had only just arrived when Reed saw him.'

'Well, he would, wouldn't he?'

Wycliffe was irritated by the inspector's complacency but he had no answer for it. 'If anybody comes forward to say they saw Barnes on the road between nine forty-five and ten, the whole case will blow up in our faces.'

'Nobody will!' Darley was aggressively final.

'I hope you're right.' Wycliffe let his pipe go out but continued to suck it moodily. The silence lengthened and Darley was getting uncomfortable.

'You think he's innocent?'

'It's possible though it's equally possible that we've got the right answer for the wrong reasons. The whole thing came too pat for my liking.'

'There are no holes in it that I can see.' Darley was patient.

'Who wrote the note about his gun?'

The inspector was ponderously reasonable. 'Somebody with no good blood for Barnes, obviously, but it was probably a lucky guess. Somebody who knew Barnes had a gun and wanted to make sure we knew too. These villages are hotbeds of gossip and backbiting.'

But Wycliffe was deeply troubled in his conscience. He was going to arrest a man of whose guilt he remained unconvinced. An introvert, he had been able to survive twenty years of dissecting his own actions and questioning his motivation, he had been able to succeed as a policeman, only because he believed that he was doing an essential job with integrity. Like every other policeman he had brought charges which failed to stick but never, either before or after a hearing, had he felt any doubt about the guilt of the accused. Now he had doubts, serious doubts, and in a case of murder. Looking at the evidence, he could find little justification for his misgivings, but it only irritated him to have Darley point this out. 'I have to *believe* in my cases,' he muttered to himself, 'and this Barnes doesn't *smell* like a murderer.' That was the rub. Wycliffe did not believe that given the circumstances all men are potential murderers. The very idea was repugnant to him. 'Killers are born,' he was fond of saying. 'Not all of them end up by killing but given the circumstances, *they will kill*; for the rest, murder is inconceivable.'

He thought enviously of the colleagues with whom he had worked during twenty years; estimable men, yet he found it difficult to believe that they had ever been troubled by ethical niceties. 'You charge a man and you do your damndest to make it stick!'

Chapter Five

At St Ives police station yesterday evening a man was charged with the murder of twenty-seven year old Anna Welles, found dead on Friday morning at her cottage in the little village of Kergwyns on the north Cornish coast . . .

'So they did get him!' Everybody pleased and just a little relieved that the law wins sometimes. Everybody except the man himself, and his wife, and Superintendent Wycliffe. But you can't please everybody.

'This case isn't over yet, don't make any mistake about that!'

Inspector Darley shrugged massive shoulders and wisely said nothing.

'The inquiry goes on; you understand?'

'As you say, sir.'

They sat opposite each other in a dingy little office at the back of the station. A dusty sunbeam from a window high up crept along the opposite wall. The superintendent's thoughts led him in a circle. A vague figure stood, just a couple of feet from Pussy Welles, facing her, holding a gun, and shot her dead. He tried to impose on that figure the form and features of Richard Barnes but he failed. The girl fell and her killer stood over her. Did he hesitate? Did he gloat? In any event, he stooped, wrenched off her shoe, reached up under her corn-flower blue dress and ripped off one stocking, lacerating her thigh. At that moment he must have looked on her with hatred, hatred so intense that the action was in the nature of an orgasmic release. Could anything stir the wretched Barnes to such a distorted emotional climax? Weak, rather ineffectual, essentially amiable – that was how he saw the man he had charged with murder.

He lit his pipe and studied his colleague over the leaping flame of the match. He had to carry Darley with him, no point in creating antagonism. 'Just to humour me, John' (the Christian name always helped), 'let's suppose for a moment that Barnes didn't do it and see where that gets us . . .'

'In Queer Street, I should think, seeing we've just locked him up!' Darley, ponderously jovial.

'It seems to me that this crime must have been the work of someone to whom violence came easily, almost naturally.'

'Why?'

Wycliffe was engagingly tentative. 'I'm not sure. I'm certainly impressed by the way in which he *exhibited* her deformity. That strikes me as the action of a man given to violence.'

'Or a timid man obsessed by fear and the hatred born of fear. The timid ones are the worst when the crunch comes.'

'You may be right, but . . .'

'Or I could imagine a jealous woman doing something of the sort.' Darley was warming, thawing out.

Wycliffe nodded. 'An interesting idea; I hadn't thought of that.' He smoked placidly as though turning the notion over in his mind. 'But it bothers me that she was shot at close range from the front with no sign of a struggle.'

'You can't defend yourself against somebody with a gun, not unless you have one too.'

'But you can try. It wouldn't be in keeping with what we know about the girl to suppose that she was petrified with fright. If somebody threatened you with a gun held only a few inches from your chest, what would you do?'

'Try to knock it up and grab it.'

'Exactly! And that's what I would expect from this full-blooded emancipated young woman. If she tried, she probably wouldn't have succeeded but she would have deflected the shot, yet the bullet entered her body horizontally, no sign of deflection.'

'He might have produced the gun and caught her unawares.'

'It's possible but unlikely; very few people are capable of shooting without hesitation – fortunately. Even with the firmest intention to kill there must be an instant when the killer screws himself up to the crucial act of pulling the trigger.'

'So?' The sunbeam in its migration now shone on Darley's bald head and he had to shield his eyes with his hand, squinting at the superintendent.

'Why don't you move?'

'What?' It would never occur to Darley to avoid discomfort but he shifted himself now, irritated by the interruption. 'How do you explain the absence of any deflection?'

Wycliffe studied the stem of his pipe as though it provided enlightenment. 'Three possibilities: she thought her assailant was playing the fool; she thought he hadn't the guts to fire; or, *she wanted to die.*'

Darley laughed. 'There's only one of those for my money. People don't play with guns in my experience and if she wanted to die it's unlikely that she would sit tight until somebody happened to come along with homicidal intentions.' He was pleased with his neat summing up. 'Which brings us back to Barnes, she wouldn't think he had the guts to fire but she was wrong.'

They sat in silence, Darley beating a little tattoo on the arm of his chair. No point in talking. Wycliffe had never found any real help in talking over a case with colleagues; he did it because it was expected. Even a painfully reasoned analysis of the facts, made in the privacy of his office, seemed to cloud rather than help his judgement. He had to let facts and ideas jostle one another in the back of his mind, on the fringe of his consciousness. He had to live in the case, soaking up the atmosphere of the place and people, then, if he was lucky, some promising notion might crystallize out. But already there had been pointed enquiries from Regional HQ. When did he expect to return?

To sit at a desk and fill out bloody forms.

Darley was growing impatient of wasted time; he picked up a copy of the case file and opened it, spreading the pages with his huge spatulate fingers. 'All right, sir! If we have to look elsewhere, what about Young, the innkeeper? If ever I saw a violent man, Young is one.'

'He hasn't got a record.'

'By the skin of his teeth! A few years back he was up on a GBH charge but the defence pleaded provocation and he got away with it. Before that he had two narrow squeaks, one for assault and the other for an offence against an under age girl. The local super doesn't like him having that licence but without an actual conviction there isn't much he can do about it.'

Darley paused, waiting for a comment but Wycliffe merely gazed at him with expressionless eyes. Darley was not put off. 'By all accounts Young was intimate with the dead girl before his accident and there's talk that he still goes there – to do the garden!' He made this seemingly innocent employment sound like a monstrous depravity. 'Then there's Dampier . . .'

'Yes, Dampier.' Wycliffe had thought a lot about him. But he had to stop Darley pricing the field. He stood up. 'I want to know more about this girl's past – about all their pasts. They're none of them locals. What brought them here? Was there any connection between any of them before they came? Start digging – there's a good fellow!' He walked to the door, picking up his stick from the corner. 'I'm going back to the village to do a bit of snooping on my own account.'

'You'll need a car.'

'Why?'

'You came in on the bus, didn't you?'

'I shall walk.'

'Walk! It'll take you the best part of an hour!'

'So what? I'm in no hurry.'

Darley shook his head slowly from side to side and watched him go.

He climbed the hill out of the town, past the new houses, past the pottery and came at last out on to the moor. A sunny April morning, warm; a moistness in the air that seemed to fix the scents of the moor, of gorse and the faintly acrid smell of decay from patches of bog. He stepped out briskly, beginning to enjoy himself. It was silent as the grave, easy to believe that there was no other living soul in the landscape.

The night before he had read Pussy Welles' novel, what there was of it, in bed. *God and Maggie Jones*. A strange uncanny story. If she had finished it there could be little doubt that she would have found a publisher. Maggie Jones, like Joan of Arc, heard voices and believed them to be of God. She was convinced that she was a divine instrument but, far from being over-awed, she regarded the relationship as a business one. 'I need Him and He needs me!' The instructions or requests which Maggie received from her exalted patron were even more partisan and parochial than St Joan's, being concerned with the welfare or downfall of individuals rather than armies or nations. And she had no hesitation in using her privileged position to secure the advancement of her friends and the confounding of her enemies. What redeemed the book from absurdity was its impudent irreverence, the piquancy of the dialogue between Him and Maggie and the Machiavellian schemes they exulted in contriving to achieve His will and purpose.

He was impressed by the book but it made him uncomfortable. If Pussy Welles got her kicks from manipulating people more or less in her power, the field must be wide. Pushed far enough even the veriest mouse may turn and fight back. Cat and Mouse! How feline can you get?

A butcher's van passed him, driven slowly, and he was aware of the scrutiny of the man at the wheel. He must be getting known in the neighbourhood or perhaps it was the oddity of seeing an obvious visitor strolling along carrying a brief-case. Scarcely realizing that he had covered the distance he found himself in the square;

the sombre grey granite looked almost mellow in the sunshine. A car, its roof-rack stacked with baggage stood outside the inn, vanguard of the army that summer would bring. Apart from the car, only two old men sunning themselves, contemplating the church-yard. He was warm and thirsty but he walked past the inn and entered the lane which led to the cliffs; he was calling on the Dampiers.

Erica took him upstairs to a room which occupied the whole of the roof-space of their bungalow. It had a magnificent dormer window overlooking the sea and it was a room after his own heart, stacked with books, littered with the impedimenta of both their trades, yet comfortable. Originals of Erica's book illustrations were propped against the walls or tacked to the slope of the ceiling. A paint stained easel, a free standing drawing board, two desks, a studio couch, chairs, bookshelves, piles of manuscript, books and always more books. A pot-bellied iron stove vented into an island chimney and the floor was covered with sisal matting and strewn with rugs.

Then there were cats. He counted six but couldn't be sure that he hadn't counted one twice or missed a couple. There was nothing patrician about these cats, they were shameless hybrid moggies but they possessed the house and carried more than their share of feline dignity because of it.

Dampier sat near the window in a rocking chair specially made for him, a cat on his knees. Seated there he looked almost normal and it was easy to forget his deformity. Wycliffe sat on the couch and Erica had a straight backed padded chair opposite her brother. She hardly took her eyes off him. She was good looking but a sharpness of feature, an air of suspicion and a scarcely veiled threat of antagonism, robbed her of beauty.

Wycliffe seemed relaxed; one of the cats jumped on to his lap and he stroked it gravely until it settled. The Dampiers waited for interrogation but instead he began to talk about children's books.

'My two were brought up on your stories,' he confided. 'They had only one fault, we couldn't get enough to satisfy the demand.'

Erica purred and Dampier was suitably confused. Dampier lit one of his cheroots and encouraged the superintendent to bring out his pipe. The thaw set in.

'So you have children, superintendent?'

'Twins, a boy and a girl, but they've gone beyond fairy stories now, I'm afraid.' Then he took a breath and plunged. He remarked on the preoccupation of children's stories with monsters, with human deformity and with beast-men. For a moment the conversation seemed to totter, then, for no obvious reason, it recovered and Dampier's self-consciousness and restraint diminished. His interest kindled. He developed a theory that childhood fascination with monstrosity is a racial memory of the palaeolithic childhood of the race, monsters envisaged in the eerie fire-lit entrances of the great limestone caves.

'Monsters and mystery are the seeds of religion and religion is the adult fairy tale,' Dampier announced. 'It emerges in each new individual as it evolved in the history of our kind.'

Wycliffe smoked placidly, apparently content to gossip. 'Yes, I suppose riddles and puzzles are as much an ingredient of children's literature as monsters. I gather that some of the less comprehensible nursery rhymes are to be interpreted as riddles and certainly a great many fairy stories centre upon the solution of a puzzle or the answer to a riddle.'

Dampier nodded. 'So, of course, do the great stories of classical mythology and this supports my recapitulation idea . . .'

'And you may add almost the whole of modern crime fiction, I suppose,' Wycliffe remarked with a grin. 'Am I right in thinking that the best writers for children have what I call a *chess* mentality, or is this a myth founded on Lewis Carroll?'

Erica had listened in silence, nodding approval from time to time, now she intervened decisively: 'Oh, it's no myth! I've always said that John has a great deal in common with Lewis Carroll. They have the same mastery of nonsensical but seemingly irrefutable logic and the same *glee* in contriving puzzles. John is an expert bridge player which is closely similar to chess in its intellectual demands and his mathematics master at school . . .'

'For God's sake, Erica!' A strangled cry of protest and pain, but with magnificent recovery of self control, Dampier went on in an almost normal voice, 'Really! To listen to Erica you might think I was a genius instead of a children's hack!'

Erica flushed and there was a moment of painful silence before she too recovered. Evidently such crises were not new to them. She turned to Wycliffe. 'Well, if you don't mind, superintendent, I'll see about the lunch.'

When she was gone Dampier apologized but Wycliffe seemed not to notice.

'Speaking of puzzles, wasn't it you who suggested that Pussy Welles might get her living from crossword puzzles?'

'Yes, it was – why?'

'She published a fair number?'

'Hundreds, I should think.'

'Wouldn't she have kept copies?'

'Of course; in fact I know that she did – several box files of them.'

'They're not there now. All we found was a few blanks.'

'How extraordinary!' Dampier was either genuinely surprised or a good actor. 'Why on earth would anybody want copies of published crosswords?'

'I've no idea.'

Dampier rocked in his chair for a moment or two, gazing out over the sea; then he swivelled round to face the superintendent. 'Look here, I know you've come to ask questions. Your little prologue has done the trick, I'm softened up so let's get on with it.'

'All right! Where were you on the night she was killed?'

Dampier smiled in spite of himself. 'So you don't really believe that Barnes did it?'

'It's my job to find the truth.'

'Then you'd better let poor old Barnes go. He's a weak mortal but he wouldn't kill a fly.' Dampier rocked to and fro. 'As to my whereabouts, there's no mystery about that, I was walking on the cliffs as I do most nights. I go out in the early morning and late at night for the obvious reason that I don't care to parade myself in daylight. It was Erica who told you chaps that I was in all the evening but I don't think they believed her.' He stopped speaking and smoked in silence for a while before asking, 'Is that all you wanted?'

'You know damn well it isn't.'

Dampier nodded. 'You want me to tell you about her.'

'And about yourself, your sister and the people who made up her circle of friends and acquaintances.'

Dampier tapped the accumulated ash from his cheroot, a long grey cylinder that dissolved into dust. 'Erica has made a life for the two of us here, a life so skilfully tailored to my deformity that sometimes I am deluded into feeling normal. Erica is one of those women with the instincts of a mother but not of a wife. If Mother Church recognized artificial insemination for spinsters Erica would be fulfilled, but instead, she mothers me. If she didn't have me it would be some other chronic invalid or hypochondriac or dogs. You understand?' He turned his blue eyes, almost childlike in their gaze on Wycliffe, tentative, afraid of being misjudged. 'I know it sounds ungrateful and ungracious but the fact that I see things pretty clearly doesn't mean that I don't appreciate what she does. The trouble is that I have the instincts of a man though I look like a caricature. I am a Toulouse Lautrec without the consolation of talent or the amenity of the brothel; not a tragedy but a bad joke.'

Wycliffe said nothing and he continued.

'I was not in love with Pussy Welles but she was necessary to me.'

'Was she in love with you?'

'You're joking!' He looked out of the window again where the scene was beginning to lose its picture postcard quality, there was a blurring of the horizon presaging rain. 'But I think she needed me too. Men don't have a monopoly of sexual aberration, superintendent.'

'So I'm told.'

Dampier laughed without humour. 'Pussy preferred cripples, which was lucky for me.' He crushed out the remains of his cheroot in the ash-tray. 'I've been frank with you because I don't want you wasting your time thinking I did it. I lose more than anyone by her death.' His face twisted in an involuntary spasm. 'I wish to God whoever shot her, shot me at the same time.' After a moment he smiled. 'That's how I feel at the moment, but I shall probably get over it.'

'Did you ever see her feet?'

'Her feet? What the hell are you at now?' He stopped. 'She certainly had a thing about her feet, she used to say she suffered from bad circulation and would never take off her ankle socks, even in bed.'

'She was deformed.'

'Rubbish!'

'She thought herself to be. She had only three toes on her left foot.'

'Well I'm damned! I never knew that.'

'The murderer did.'

Dampier was watching the sea once more. He must have known its every mood. Grey smoky clouds were climbing up the sky reaching out for the sun. 'It's difficult for me to be objective about her, she was a strange girl. She had a thirst for power which I imagine is uncommon among women. She exploited the power of her sex and I think she got a kick out of her crosswords mainly because she was determining how several thousand people would spend two or three hours of their leisure. I know it sounds fantastic but that was how she thought. I remember her saying to me once: "I wish I had pots of money, John." I asked her what she would do with it and she smiled. "I haven't thought but I'd get a hell of a kick making my will!" Another time, apropos of nothing, she said, "It is simple to gain control over another human being; all you have to do is to discover his weakness. Everybody has one, a tender spot, a heel of Achilles; find it and you are in the saddle." I asked her if she had such a weakness and she laughed. "Of course! But I take damn good care not to let anybody know about it!" '

'Was she happy?'

Dampier looked at him in surprise. 'Does it sound as though she was? For that matter, who is? Certainly not the ones who are cursed with an insatiable desire for new experiences and sensations. In my opinion she never knew a moment of contentment let alone of happiness. The best she knew was a pleasurable excitement which quickly yielded to disappointment. She could *not* be satisfied, it was not in her nature, so that her only pleasure came in anticipation.'

'Did you ever hear her speak of death – her own death?'

Dampier hesitated. 'I think you mean, did she contemplate suicide? Of course, I don't know, but she said a strange thing to me once. The circumstances you can imagine; she said, "I wonder what it will be like to strip away this eighth veil of our flesh? Will it mean death or release?" '

'What did your sister think of her?'

'What would you expect? She hated her. But I think she looked upon her as a sort of prophylactic medicine for me. She was made welcome here and everything was friendly on the surface.'

Wycliffe rested his hands on his knees and seemed to study his fingers. He spoke without looking at Dampier. 'When her body was found it was fully clothed except for her left shoe and stocking which were missing. Her deformed foot was exposed and there were scratches suggesting that the stocking had been removed with considerable violence after death.'

'And you think little Barnes did that?'

'What do you think?'

'That it must have been a woman.'

Wycliffe said nothing, allowing the full implication to sink in. Two or three times Dampier started to speak then changed his mind. The seconds ticked by.

'What about the others?' Wycliffe asked.

It seemed to be a relief for Dampier to talk about the Barneses, the Mitfords, Lomax, the innkeeper and the queers but he had little of interest to say. It was evident that he liked the Barneses but he had a strong antipathy to the Mitfords.

'School teachers! Janice is all Cheltenham Ladies' and Young Conservative while Alfred is convinced that he was singled out by providence to mould the minds and bodies of the young. Poor devil! I think she'd given up hope when she hooked him.'

'They don't sound like congenial company for Pussy Welles.'

Dampier agreed. 'But I think Alfred's unassailable pomposity was a challenge to her.'

'Do you think he resisted successfully?'

Dampier grinned. 'If Janice got to know that he didn't your murder would be solved.'

Wycliffe left Dampier standing at the gate, a cat perched on his crooked shoulder, another nuzzling at his legs. What to make of him? Deeply conscious of his deformity, he had the strength to come to terms with it, to smother his bitterness and to live a life as normal as intelligence and an iron will could make it. He was armoured against the world, but if someone –

a woman – pierced that armour, kindling emotions it was designed to shield . . . If Pussy Welles got her kicks from manipulating people, Dampier was terrifyingly vulnerable and highly dangerous. A man with nothing to lose.

Chapter Six

The church clock chimed the quarter; a quarter past twelve. Time for a drink before lunch. The bar was empty except for the landlord reading his paper, spread on the counter. He seemed to be a fixture at this time of day. Wycliffe asked for a light ale and took it to a table by the window, anxious to avoid conversation, but the landlord didn't want to talk either. Wycliffe was still thinking of the Dampiers. People who earned their living by any sort of freelance creative work intrigued him, perhaps he had romantic notions about them. At any event, he envied them their freedom, even their fundamental insecurity. He had always had a literary bent; if things had been otherwise when he left schoool . . . if he had taken his chance of university. But the twins had made it. Which reminded him that he had promised to ring his wife. He was on his way to the telephone in the lobby when he met Darley coming in, Darley looking glum.

'The money's been found.'

'What money?'

'The hundred quid in tenners which Barnes hid in the hedge.'

'So he did hide it?'

Darley nodded. They moved back to the super-intendent's table.

'Drink?'

'I'll have a tonic water, thanks.' He removed his trilby and placed it carefully on the bench beside him. 'Last night, one of the car patrols up near the border picked up an old tramp – Jimmy Ellis – drunk and disorderly and they found forty quid in tenners on him. This morning, when he's sobered up, he admitted having another fifty stashed away.'

'Did he say where he got it?'

'From a hole in the hedge on the coast road near Kergwyns.' Darley spoke with disgust. 'There's an old tumbled down shack by the roadside and Jimmy was preparing to doss down for the night when he saw a car stop, a man got out and hid something in the hedge. Of course, when the car drove off, Jimmy took a look and he found the notes. Surprisingly enough he's pretty definite about time. He knows it was Thursday and he says the church clock had struck ten three or four minutes before. Having got this windfall, Jimmy was too scared to spend it but when he got away up the other end of the county he began to feel safer and temptation was too strong for him.'

'He didn't by any chance see the fellow hide a gun in the culvert?'

'No such luck! The culvert is only fifty yards down the road so he would have been sure to see if there was anything to be seen. Actually he says that he waited for the lights of the car to disappear before he started to investigate.'

Wycliffe shrugged. 'Well! That doesn't help the case against Barnes.' He stopped abruptly and looked at Darley. 'Have you got something else up your sleeve?'

Darley was sheepish. 'I'm afraid so. Ellis says the same car – a red Mini – passed him on the road a quarter of an hour earlier, going in the opposite direction – that is, towards Kergwyns.'

The superintendent sighed. 'So that's that!'

'I've no doubt he could be shaken. I mean, red Minis . . .'

'Rubbish! This lets Barnes out and you know it!'

The bar was filling, several locals and a few obvious visitors. Wycliffe said, 'Let's get out of here!'

They strolled along the path towards the cliffs. 'We've been taken for a ride! I was afraid of it. Barnes was framed. That girl deliberately involved him in a murder charge.'

Darley was satirical. 'Her own! She frames Barnes for her own murder – it's ingenious and I doubt if it's been done before.'

But Wycliffe was in no mood for banter. 'Look at the facts, man! At a quarter to ten, just a few minutes before she died, Pussy Welles telephoned her friend, Elsa Cooper, to tell her that she was pregnant, that Barnes was the father of her child and that he was with her discussing what they should do. It's an unlikely story at best. Why did she ring the Cooper woman?'

Darley was nettled. 'She rang, because she wanted to protect herself from Barnes by telling someone else the facts *in his presence*.'

'But he wasn't there!'

'We've only the word of a drink sodden old tramp for that.'

'And Barnes' own word – don't forget that. It's corroboration we've got now, and disinterested corroboration. If Barnes arrived at the cottage when he says he did, then he didn't kill her. But that telephone call to Elsa Cooper and the one to Barnes himself, fixed him with both motive and opportunity;

the means was his anyway. Admittedly, he made things blacker for himself by going off with the money and hiding it, but remember, there is no evidence that he hid the gun.'

'I can't believe that the girl rigged her own murder.' Darley was doggedly obstinate.

'I could believe almost anything of that girl but that doesn't alter the situation as far as Barnes is concerned. We've no case.'

Darley looked at the superintendent curiously. 'You sound pleased.'

Wycliffe nodded. 'I am; though God knows why.'

They had reached the end of the lane and stood among the bracken facing out over a sparkling sea, but neither of them saw it.

'They'll be serving lunch; come back and have some with me.'

But Darley was not to be wooed. 'No thanks. If what you say is true, we're back to square one and I've got work to do – sir.'

'Suit yourself.'

They walked back in silence for a while then Wycliffe said, 'Pussy Welles' husband fell over a cliff, one of her lovers met with a curious road accident that was almost fatal, now Pussy herself has been murdered and another of her lovers framed for the crime. All this in a little over five years – it's too much!'

'I don't see what you're getting at.'

'Neither do I but I don't like it.'

Outside the inn, Wycliffe said, 'I shall be at the cottage this afternoon if you want me.'

'Doing what?'

'I've no idea. Snooping, brooding.'

'We've been over that place . . .'

'. . . with a fine tooth comb – I know. Anyway, don't let me keep you.'

He enjoyed his lunch; lentil soup, chicken with half a bottle of white wine, apple tart and cream. Good plain food, well cooked, that was what he liked. The dining-room was more than half full and Sylvie had her work cut out but she made sure he wasn't kept waiting. 'When are you going to let that poor man go?' she whispered as she changed the plates. He gave her a black look but she only winked.

Afterwards, feeling a little drowsy, he walked out into the watery sunshine, along the unsurfaced lane to the cottage, without seeing a soul. He unlocked the glass panelled door and entered the little white porch with its telephone. The tulips were still on the telephone table, dropping now, their petals all over the floor. He still hadn't spoken to his wife; he dialled.

'Is that you, dear?'

Who else?

'You sound dreadfully tired; don't overdo it.' His wife was convinced that he overworked. What would Darley have said?

'The twins? They've gone to Sidmouth this after-noon. They both hope your case will be over soon so that you can spend a bit of time with them before they go back . . .'

Using Pussy Welles' phone, he couldn't help trying to make comparisons between her and Helen; they were both women but there the resemblance seemed to end.

' 'Bye, love, see you soon.'

He went into the sitting-room. The charcoal outline and the stains were still there. Already the cottage smelt of mustiness and disuse and it was chilly. He looked round at the unconcealing furniture on stilt legs, at the spread of carpet and at the formal prints on the walls, and shook his head. He passed into the kitchen; stainless steel and laminated plastic; a dining alcove with seats for four, a radio on a ledge and over it a framed abstract glowing in reds and orange.

About as personal as an operating theatre.

But he explored the drawers and cupboards of the kitchen fittings, finding only expected things; though there was a red covered account book; a detailed record of her housekeeping expenses; separate sections for milk and bread, paid for by the week; and for goods from the village store, paid for by the month. Difficult to reconcile this careful housekeeper with the improvident wanton, living on her wits. But perhaps even whores keep accounts.

He dropped the book back into a drawer and started to poke about in the coke boiler. A heavy tarry deposit round the flue suggested that someone had burned a great deal of paper. 'And cleaned the thing out afterwards,' Wycliffe muttered. It must have been recent, a good coke fire would have shifted it. For some reason, most of the records of her work were missing, her letters and the host of personal papers that one accumulates. Had they been burned here? It seemed likely. By the murderer? Hardly. It would have been too big a risk and taken too long. In any case, why should he burn her business papers? And if so much had to go, why leave the few crossword blanks? Why leave the manuscript of her novel? Wycliffe was convinced that there had been deliberate selection; equally convinced that it had been made by Pussy Welles, herself. What was left was intended to speak for her, or at least *of* her in a particular way. Did this mean that she expected to be murdered? Incredibly, it seemed so and this tied in with her attempt to implicate Barnes.

Wycliffe had the tantalizing feeling that he was skirmishing on the fringe of the truth. An image had formed in his mind but it was blurred and indistinct, it would not focus. He knew from experience that it was no good trying too hard. He climbed the twisted little stair, only glanced into the bedroom, and entered her study. Here, if anywhere, she belonged; despite her reputation he believed that her broadest contact with life was on the plane of the intellect. Perhaps he was unduly influenced by her novel.

Afternoon sunshine flooded the little room and it needed no great effort of the imagination to see her seated at the desk, the sun glinting on her auburn hair, turning up references, filling in clues, her forehead puckered in a frown of concentration. Was it more or less difficult to imagine her on the other side of the partition, wrestling with her hunchback on the bed or cynically tempting another of her lovers to the limit of erotic abandonment? He believed that the disparate elements of her personality came nearest to reconciliation when she was sitting at this desk, recording the outrageous activities of Maggie Jones. Did she chuckle at her own audacity? Wycliffe thought not. Pussy rarely chuckled or laughed; an occasional smile, a Mona Lisa smile.

He perched himself on the edge of the desk and surveyed the room. Books. They were a literary lot in this case. And she had catholic interests, everything from archaeology to literary criticism, from modern poetry to the theory of games. He snooped, picking out a book here and there, and so he came upon a little nest of erotic works; nothing special about them except that they were all inscribed on the flyleaf, some with amatory message, others without, but all, *From A.* Alfred Mitford? Perhaps. The dates spread over two years and the last was three years old. Each of the books he examined, he held by the covers and shook the pages, gathering only a bus ticket, two anonymous scraps of paper and a receipted bill. He sat down in the armchair by the desk and started again, just gazing blankly at the books, the walls, the floor, the records . . .

The only pictures were a few framed photographs; they might be interpreted as trophies, but there was no knowing how Pussy regarded them. A profile of Dampier which looked as though it had been enlarged from a snapshot; probably he would never agree to a photograph. A portrait of Lomax, seated at his desk, pen in hand, Rembrandt lighting. Very distinguished. A photograph of Mike Young, barely recognizable; a slimmer, younger, undamaged version; undoubtedly he had what used to be called sex appeal. And a picture of Mitford; Mitford standing in front of a rakish looking sports car, holding a cup. The picture must have been taken several years ago; at least there was no sign of his present, well matured pot belly. Wycliffe took the pictures down and laid them on the desk. In doing so, he noticed that the one of Mitford was bulkier than the others, there was something between the picture and the backing and the sealing tape was new. He ripped it off, lifted out the millboard backing and uncovered a little pad of folded newspaper cuttings which he spread on the desk.

FATAL FALL AT CLEGAR
Death of St Ives Business Man
A verdict of accidental death was recorded by the

Coroner, Dr J. L. Goody, on Mr Samuel Arthur Horner of 26 Rush Street, St Ives, at an inquest on Friday. Mr Horner fell 200 feet to his death from the notorious Clegar Cliff while bird watching on the evening of the 6th September.

In evidence it was stated that Mr Horner had formed the habit of strolling along the cliffs on fine evenings with his binoculars, watching the seabirds coming in to roost on the ledges. One witness said that he had frequently observed Mr Horner to stand dangerously near the edge in his efforts to obtain a better view. Mr Horner's body was not recovered until the following day.

Newcomers to St Ives

Mr Horner, who was 32, was a comparative newcomer to St Ives having started the business in Rush Street only six months ago, after moving from London with his wife. Mrs Horner said that she had often been concerned at her husband's apparent indifference to danger when he was absorbed in his hobby. The coroner expressed deep sympathy with the widow and hoped that the tragedy might serve to remind other coastal bird watchers of the risks attendant on over enthusiastic pursuit of their hobby.

The other two cuttings were more recent and dealt with Young's car smash:

LICENSEE IN CAR SMASH
Serious Accident on Coast Road

On Friday night at a little before eleven, Mr Michael Young, licensee of The Inn at Kergwyns was driving homewards from St Ives when his car skidded at Kitt's Corner. Mr Young was thrown through the windscreen and received multiple injuries. He is now undergoing treatment at the Royal County Hospital where his condition is reported to be 'serious'.

Mr Young might have lain unconscious at the scene of the accident for several hours but for an anonymous telephone call to the police.

Mystery of Anonymous Call

The police are unable to offer any explanation of the anonymous call but inquiries are proceeding. There are no houses in the immediate vicinity of the crash and during the winter months hardly any traffic on the road after nightfall. The nearest public telephone is situated in the square at Kergwyns, one and a half miles away but the police are convinced that the call was made within minutes of the crash. It is understood that the voice of the caller was distorted as though by an attempt at disguise.

Oil on the Road

The accident appears to have been caused by the presence of a large quantity of motor oil on the road. A five gallon drum, almost empty, was found at some distance from the smash and appears to have been struck by the car. The police are investigating the possibility that the drum fell from a passing lorry but so far their inquiries have been unrewarding.

Mr Young has been licensee of the Kergwyns Inn for five years and is well known to all football

*enthusiasts as the energetic chairman of the Pen-
with Club.*

The final cutting was a paragraph only:

KERGWYNS ACCIDENT

*The motor accident to Mr Michael Young,
licensee of the Kergwyns Inn, reported in our last
week's issue, remains something of a mystery. The
police have been unable to trace the anonymous
caller who notified them of the accident or to
discover the source of the oil on the road which
caused the accident. Chief Inspector Judd of the
County CID stated that there was no suspicion
of foul play.*

*Mr Young is reported to be making slow
progress towards recovery.*

Wycliffe read the accounts slowly, carefully. There
could be no doubt that the cuttings had been deliberately hidden in the picture; but why? Anybody could
go to the newspaper office and look them up. To make
sure, he removed the other photographs from their
frames but found nothing. He piled them together on
the desk, except Mitford's which he slipped into his
case, and got up to leave. It was then that he noticed
someone in the little walled garden below. At first he
thought it was someone hiding, for the figure which
he had only glimpsed had disappeared behind a laurel
bush but he was soon disillusioned, the innkeeper
emerged into sight, calmly hoeing round the shrubs.
There was no reason why he shouldn't; the place
belonged to him and although the police held the keys
of the cottage they had placed no ban on the garden.

Still, it seemed a trifle provocative. He would go down and see what Young had to say for himself. But on his way downstairs, the telephone rang. It was Darley.

'A bit more information from the Yard. On Lomax. He was Pussy Welles' sugar daddy when she worked in London, the chap who, according to Elsa Cooper, used to give her expensive presents.'

'Lomax!'

'Exactly. You never can tell. He was a lecturer, as he said, and she worked in the Registry. To cut a long story short he seems to have lost his head completely and when she let him down with a bump, he took to drink and finally had to resign. That's when he came down here. According to the Yard, he's a bit of a joke in zoological circles with his research on lemmings . . .'

'On what?'

'Lemmings. Apparently his life's work is concerned with social behaviour in lemmings but it never comes to anything. Meanwhile he makes a pretty good living writing popular natural history. I gather it's all a bit pathetic . . .'

'I don't know about pathetic but he was very foolish not to come clean. I think I'd better have a chat with Mr Lomax.'

'I somehow thought you might. Shall I have him brought in?'

'Wycliffe hesitated. 'No, we'll keep it on a friendly basis for the moment.'

He forgot Young in the garden and had locked the front door when he remembered. He was tempted to leave it but bitter experience had taught him not to ignore anything in the slightest degree unusual so he went back through the house.

Young was unperturbed. 'I've always kept an eye on

the place; gardening wasn't much in her line and she was glad for me to come along and keep it tidy.' He held his head so that the good side of his face was towards the superintendent, giving the disturbing impression that he was speaking to someone else.

'It's my cottage, as I told you, my father and mother lived here after they retired until they died and I suppose I shall move in when I've finished over yonder.' He nodded in the direction of the inn. He rested one enormous hand on the hoe and though he spoke amiably enough, his hand seemed to twitch as though impatient for some violent activity.

'I was surprised to see you here,' Wycliffe said, shortly. 'There's no reason why you shouldn't continue to look after the garden but you mustn't attempt to get into the house until we hand over the keys. You understand?'

'You can rely on me, I've no call to want to go in there.' His manner became insinuating. 'How's the case going, superintendent? Dr Barnes is a nice enough young fellow and I can't really believe he did it. Do you think he did, sir?'

'He's been charged,' Wycliffe snapped. Then he changed the subject abruptly. 'About your accident.'

'My accident?' Young was not only surprised but uneasy.

'Are you satisfied that it was an accident?'

'Of course it was! I don't understand what you're getting at, superintendent.' No mistaking his alarm now.

'You didn't receive a warning?'

'A warning?'

'A warning that you might have such an accident.'

He was breathing hard and his hands were restless. He said nothing for some time then he made a sudden movement. 'You mean a premonition.' He laughed. 'I don't believe in that sort of thing.'

'Neither do I!' Wycliffe snapped. 'I'm talking about a warning, a threat if you like.'

The innkeeper looked straight at him now and his expression was ludicrous. 'I don't know what you're talking about!' He tried to sound truculent but he wasn't in full control of his voice.

Wycliffe spoke lightly. 'I think you understand me perfectly. Just think it over. It may not be healthy to keep secrets for too long.'

'That sounds like a threat to me.'

Wycliffe's temper flared. 'Don't be a bigger fool than God made you! If you didn't get a warning the first time, I'm giving you one now.'

Young made no response; he continued to rest on the hoe, staring away from the superintendent.

'You mentioned your parents just now, I understood that you were adopted.'

Young faced round and regarded Wycliffe with his good eye. 'That's right.'

'How old were you when you were adopted?'

'Eight.'

'What happened to your real father and mother?'

'I can't remember, perhaps I never knew.'

'Did your foster parents have this pub when they adopted you?'

He seemed more nervous than ever but his answers were straightforward. 'No, they had an off-licence in Ealing; they bought this place and came down here to live when I was twelve. They wanted to live in the country.'

'What was your name before you were adopted, Mr Young?'

He raised his shoulders irritably. 'I can't remember. If you had the sort of childhood I had you would try to forget it.'

Wycliffe moved off towards the cottage but the innkeeper called him back. His manner had become conspiratorial. 'I'll show you something, here against the wall.' At the foot of the wall, lying beside a mound of rotting leaves was the body of a cat, a Siamese; fur was missing in patches and the body was beginning to show signs of decay. 'It was her cat, I came across it by accident, buried under that pile of leaves.'

'This afternoon?'

'Yes. Whatever you might think, superintendent, I haven't been near this garden until this afternoon since she died.'

'All right, no need to get excited. Have you got a bag we can put it in?'

Young seemed disposed to continue his protestations but changed his mind. 'There may be something in here.'

Wycliffe followed him into a small lean-to built against the garden wall. It was dark, damp and earthy; when his eyes got used to the light he could see a bag of fertilizer propped up on a couple of blocks, shelves with flower pots and a jumble of tins and bottles. 'Was she troubled by rats?'

'I shouldn't think so – why?'

Wycliffe held up a rusted tin of rat poison, a branded product.

'I shouldn't think there were any rats about now but there might have been a year or two back when they had horses next door. There used to be a stables the other side of this wall but it's all derelict now.' He held out a large plastic bag that had once contained fertilizer, 'Will this do?'

They put the cat in the bag and Wycliffe went off with his trophy. But it was not the dead cat that occupied his mind. Four names chased each other round and round: Horner, Young, Pussy Welles and Barnes. Two were dead, one was grossly disfigured and one was in gaol on a murder charge. Isolated misfortunes? Or a closely knit pattern? And something even vaguer troubled him – a resemblance which he had noticed yet now eluded recollection.

Back in the square, two small boys and a girl played with a ball and Wycliffe watched them with satisfaction. The almost total lack of overt activity in the little village was beginning to get him down. It was like a film set between takes.

Lomax lived in a house immediately behind the church, reached by a track which left the road from the village just beyond the square. Wycliffe loped along between high hedges without even a glimpse of the church tower to remind him of the proximity of the village. It was so quiet, he could hear cows ripping off grass in a hidden field and a bumble bee, busy with the primroses, sounded like an aeroplane. After a little while a farm gate, painted white, straddled the path and admitted him to the cobbled courtyard of the house. It had once been a farmyard but now sedums and sea-pinks grew between the cobbles and a Cornish Cross had been erected on a granite plinth in the middle. A black and white cat, sitting in the sunshine, stopped licking its paws to watch. He rang the bell on the house door. No answer. He tried again. Silence. He crossed the yard to a large outbuilding, pushed open the wicket and entered a semi-darkness alive with muted rustlings, squeaks and twitterings. The lemmings. As the superintendent's eyes accommodated to the dimness he could see a great battery of wire cages each about eighteen inches cube and housing one or a pair of lemmings. He watched them aimlessly for a while and they took notice of him, some of them posturing aggressively, rising on their hind legs, grunting and squeaking. The cages took up only a fraction of the shed space which was otherwise empty except for a wheelbarrow, gardening tools and bins for the lemmings' food. An area of oil stained floor indicated where Lomax kept his car.

A nervous, querulous voice demanded, 'Who's there?' So he went out, apologizing.

'What were you doing in there?' Lomax seemed really agitated, but Wycliffe soothed him.

'I've had such a lot of trouble with my animals recently.'

'Trouble?'

'Deaths unrelated to age.' Lomax nodded jerkily; all his movements were jerky, bird-like. 'I can't account for it. In all the years I've reared these creatures, I've never encountered anything like it and I keep the fullest demographic records . . .'

'I'm here to talk about Pussy Welles, Mr Lomax.'

He looked hurt, a little shocked at the interruption but he nodded. 'Yes, of course, you must come inside.'

The inside of the house surprised Wycliffe, it had turned into a modern villa with all the trimmings and Lomax displayed it with pleasure and pride. 'I live alone of course, and I do most things for myself, just a woman from the village three half days a week . . .'

One room occupied the whole of the front of the

house downstairs and looked out on a lawn bordered with shrubs and surrounded by a high wall. The garden adjoined the churchyard but only the tower and the wind blasted sycamores appeared above the wall. The room had been equipped and arranged to present its owner as a scholar, a *savant*. Glass fronted shelves of gleaming mahogany held volumes of *Proceedings* and *Transactions* of a dozen learned societies; box files in neat rows were labelled with subject cards, a recessed bench held an impressive microscope and lighting devices and a polished table near the window was clear except for writing materials and a pile of galley proofs. All that was needed was that he should sit in the padded leather chair, take up his pen and be ready for the photograph that would appear first in *Nature* and later, perhaps, in his biography. *Dr Edgar Lomax at work in his study.* What strange carrots lure us donkeys on!

'This is where I work.'

But when they were seated he reverted to Pussy Welles of his own accord. 'I miss her, superintendent. She was a remarkable girl. You would be surprised at the subjects we discussed – everything . . . And she could listen . . .' His vagueness measured his difficulty in defining let alone filling the gap in his life.

Had Pussy Welles submitted to boredom by this man? Or did she get some sort of kick out of the unlikely association? At every turn it was the enigma of her character which clouded the emerging outlines of his ideas and reduced them once more to flux. It was easy to feel sorry for Lomax but there was more to it than that.

'Why didn't you tell me that you knew her in London?'

'So you found out.' He nodded in acceptance of the inevitable. 'I had to resign. I behaved very badly, but she was cruel. It is strange that running through her kindness, her patience and her generosity, there was this vein of cruelty – of sadism.'

'But you followed her down here?'

A wry smile. 'I had to.'

Wycliffe said nothing and after a moment Lomax felt driven to fill the silence. 'I never deceived myself that she loved me but she was the nearest I ever came to . . . to . . .' He searched for a word and failed to find one. 'I was never a good mixer. Even at school I was the boy who lurked in the corner of the playground half hoping for friendly notice, half afraid of being laughed at or bullied.' He smiled selfconsciously. 'You can imagine that I never made a hit with girls. Until I met her I had never known what it was to possess a woman. That amused and attracted her.' He took out a handkerchief and patted his forehead and lips which glistened with sweat. 'You will understand that I was in no position to lay down conditions, I could not afford the luxury of jealousy.'

Wycliffe was touched and shamed at the spectacle of such humility. There is something profoundly wrong with a society which fails to educate its youth in the things that really matter. But he was a suspect.

'Who killed her?'

Lomax was not taken by surprise. 'I told you before that in my view, suicide is the most likely explanation of her death. She was deeply unhappy.' He was dissatisfied with this statement and searched for words to express himself more precisely. 'Unhappy is not the word, she was plagued by a gnawing discontent . . . I can't explain it but anyone who knew her was aware of it.'

Dampier had said, 'In my opinion she never knew a moment of contentment . . .'

'You knew her husband?'

'Only vaguely; he was a member of the local natural history society. An amiable, quiet man, he seemed to be. As a matter of fact, I used to wonder why she married him.'

'You thought you would have made a better match?' Cruelty to dumb animals.

'No, I did not think that. I wondered if she had married him for the same reason as she . . . associated with me.'

'And what was that?' Crucify him! It's all in the sacred name of justice.

'I hinted at it just now. I think that she took pleasure in broadening one's experience of the – ah – erotic aspects of love. If it didn't sound absurd coming from a middle-aged man, I would almost say that she took pleasure in the corruption of innocence.' He was obviously distressed but, apparently determined to tell the truth as he saw it. 'I know this sounds ungrateful but she was, as I have said, a complex personality.'

Wycliffe had left his chair and walked over to one of the bookcases. He had his back to Lomax, scanning the titles. Give him back a grain of self respect. 'Your relationship with her must also have been more complex than you suggest.'

'In what way?'

'Well, you shared certain intellectual interests.'

'Yes. That is true; that is very true.'

'I see you have a copy of *Cook's Psychology of Deformity*.'

118

Lomax answered with apparent casualness. 'Yes, the subject interests me, why?'

'I happened to notice a copy of the same book on Dampier's shelves.'

'Which shouldn't surprise you, surely!' Lomax said.

Chapter Seven

The curtains were drawn over the great window of the Dampiers' upstair room and some of the stuff that usually cluttered the floor had been cleared. Three card tables with chairs round them were set for Mah-Jongg, the walls of tiles already built and the counters apportioned. The old iron stove in the centre of the room cast its orange glow and roared in competition with the gale outside. Spring had slipped back into winter in a single day as it is apt to do, and the wind came from the north, a bitterly cold breath from the Arctic sea. John Dampier sat in the firelight waiting for his guests while Erica busied herself downstairs. His massive ungainly body fitted the rocking chair so that it seemed part of him and he rocked to and fro, smoking one of his cheroots and stroking the sleeping cat on his lap. He was experiencing a rare contentment. For the most part, his waking hours seemed to be a struggle against boredom, against frustration and against the crushing burden of his deformity, but now and then, for no reason that he could tell, he would find himself unexpectedly at peace, not only resigned but content. It was like coming in from a storm and shutting the door. He wished that he was spending the evening alone but his serenity was too deep to be unduly disturbed. He wondered vaguely what Wycliffe was playing at.

On his second visit, the superintendent had been decidedly less amiable, at least to begin with, but when he was leaving he said, 'You haven't thought of having another of your Mah-Jongg evenings?'

'No. In any case, it's too soon; nobody would come.'

'They would if they knew I was interested.'

'You want me to lay on something?'

'It might help.'

'A bit unorthodox, surely?'

'So is murder.'

'At least it means that he doesn't suspect you,' Erica said when he told her.

'Of course, it means nothing of the sort!' It had been his own first thought but it irritated him to have her put it into words.

'In any case, you've nothing to fear,' she said in self reassurance.

Nothing to fear. It was true that he was not afraid but that was because he had so little to lose – less now. It was one of his few compensations that he could view the worst with equanimity. For a man without belief there is only death to fear and he was certainly unafraid of death; sometimes it seemed to beckon him kindly, as a friend, a promise, not a threat. He would look down from a cliff edge at the dim mysterious water and wonder why he bothered to cling to life. He knew why – because it was interesting, though less so now that Pussy was gone. She had been an unfailing source of surprise, even on that last day – her last.

It was that day the superintendent wanted to know about.

'It was a Thursday – *your* day, wasn't it, Mr Dampier?'

Nasty! But true. All the village knew that. Bit by bit,

without much need for persuasion, Wycliffe got the story – most of it.

He had walked along the cliff then struck inland arriving, as usual at the back door of the cottage. Not that he cared about people knowing but he hated to be stared at. It was four o'clock and they chatted, then had tea. And after tea, bed. It was their routine. When it was over and they were lying side by side, recapturing the perspectives of normality, she said, 'I'm pregnant, John, and it's yours.'

He was surprised but not unduly concerned. Her particular brand of sensuality demanded risk and he had considered the possibility.

'I'll make arrangements for you to go into a clinic in town.'

'No. I want you to marry me.' Just like that. He was astounded.

'Erica will have to go, of course,' she added, an apparent afterthought.

Then he understood – or thought he did. 'There's no question of Erica being forced out of her own home.'

'Don't fret yourself; she'll go of her own accord.'

'I wouldn't count on that.'

She got out of bed and stood, naked, stroking her belly and smiling. 'When she realizes that the alternative is an abortion which will destroy your child, she'll go fast enough. Erica couldn't live with that thought to plague her. Your child, even by me, will be sacrosanct.' Anger or hatred suddenly flared. 'My God! If it wasn't for her conventional little mind she would be in bed with you herself!'

And that was as far as Wycliffe could persuade him to go.

'You believed that she really intended to marry you?'

'At the time.'

'And since?'

'I've had doubts.'

'What happened after that?'

'I've said all I intend to say.'

'I can't accept reservations in a murder case, Mr Dampier.'

'You can go to hell!'

It wsn't obstinacy or even self preservation, he could not bring himself to admit that for once his armour had been pierced and emotions roused which he had long believed dead. He would not order his thoughts to reconstruct those moments of anger and humiliation.

Wycliffe had stared in silence for some time, then: 'Very well! But if the charge against Barnes is withdrawn you may be forced to answer my questions.'

Then he made his proposition – a Mah-Jongg party – it sounded bizarre, put like that.

The door bell.

Ten minutes past seven. Curiosity (or apprehension?) had so far overcome good manners as to bring somebody twenty minutes early. Erica would be annoyed, she was still preparing refreshments. He wondered if Ursula Barnes would come; he had seen her only once since her husband's arrest and she had been tight, resentful, antagonistic, just as Erica would have been. Everybody to blame. Women are irrational animals. But it looked as though she wouldn't have to suffer much longer.

The early arrival was Janice Mitford; he might have known. He could hear her high pitched chatter, always on the fringe of hysteria, and Erica's cool replies. Where was Alfred? Of course, he might be there without having spoken yet.

But Alfred wasn't there, she came up the stairs alone.

'Hullo, John, I came early because I wanted the chance of a word before the others come.'

She had cultivated what was supposed to be an easy companionable manner with men which raised his hackles. Bloody bitch! What he had against her was nebulous; she led Alfred a dance but he despised Alfred. The real trouble was that she didn't know how to behave like a woman and she groped desperately, disastrously, to find out. One ought to be sorry for her but instead she had the impact of an ill-timed joke.

'Do you mind if I switch on the lights? I can't stand the semi-darkness.'

She sat in the chair opposite him, shooing off one of the cats. The Mah-Jongg evenings had never been occasions for dressing up but her jumper and slacks were something new. The V-neck and the clinging thin wool advertised what was underneath.

'I'm worried, John, desperately worried!' She lowered her voice. 'In fact, I'm frightened and I've nobody to turn to but you.' She blinked rapidly, touching her eyes with a rolled up handkerchief. 'It's Alfred, he's in some sort of trouble over Pussy Welles.'

Dampier shifted impatiently in his chair so that the cat on his lap stretched and clawed the air once or twice before settling down again. Perhaps she was frightened but he was damned if he was going to be comforting.

She drew a packet of cigarettes from her handbag, tapped one nervously on the packet and forced Dampier to disturb the cat once more in order to light it. 'I'm a bundle of nerves, John; sometimes I hardly know what I'm doing!' She smoked with frequent short inhalations until the cigarette had a quarter gone, then she crushed it out in the ash-tray. It seemed that she had screwed herself up to the pitch of courage.

'It started with her coming to the house on the afternoon of the day she was killed. I was out in the back garden and when I came in he was talking to her in the porch. Of course, she soon went but it was obvious that what she said to him was upsetting. The next day when we heard she had been shot, he just went to pieces. He wouldn't eat and he couldn't sleep and he wouldn't tell me what was wrong. The last couple of days he seemed to be getting over it but this morning, Inspector Darley came and he's as bad as ever again. Really, John, I don't know what to do. Thank God it isn't term time.'

Dampier regarded her without compassion. 'You think Alfred might have killed her — is that what's worrying you?'

The fright in her eyes was unmistakably genuine. 'Good God, no!' She put a hand to her mouth. 'I never said that. I just want to know what hold she had over him that even now she's dead puts him in such a panic.'

'Somebody killed her,' Dampier said, 'and even the police are beginning to realize it wasn't Barnes, but it must have been one of our little set.'

She looked at him wide eyed, on the brink of hysteria but she controlled herself. 'This is awful! I don't know what to do!' She had her knuckles in her mouth like a child trying to hold back tears.

'Is Alfred coming?'

She looked at him vaguely and he had to repeat the question.

'Of course he's coming. I came early because I wanted to talk to you, now I wish I hadn't.'

The door bell again. Janice got out her make-up and set about repairing the ravages. 'Heavens! I look a sight.'

This time it was Mike Young. His low pitched

guttural speech was unmistakable. He came upstairs heavily like a desperately tired man, and when he spoke he seemed to have trouble finding the words and enunciating them. Dampier wondered if he had had a mild stroke until he realized that he was merely drunk.

'Glad you were able to come, Mike.'

Young nodded. 'It seemed like a bloody command performance so I thought I couldn't afford to miss it.' He slumped heavily into a chair. Hitherto he had maintained a vulgar smartness in his dress – fancy waist-coats and check suits, now he looked seedy, his clothes creased and soiled. He took a packet of cigarettes from his pocket and lit one with the precision of a drunken man, then he seemed to notice Janice for the first time.

'Hullo! Where's Alfred? Isn't he coming?'

She looked at him with annoyance and distaste; his use of their Christian names had been a sore point for a long time and she had blamed it on Alfred. ('You never know how to keep your distance with people!') But she answered Young civilly, 'He's coming later – why?'

Young shrugged. 'I feel sorry for him, that's all.'

'Why should you feel sorry for my husband?'

He shook his head and laughed as though at a very good joke.

Janice stared at him and her mouth slackened, she might have screamed if Dampier hadn't cut in, not angry, but authoritative, 'You're drunk, Mike! Either you behave or you get out!'

The tension evaporated. Young mumbled an apology, Janice controlled herself and Dampier felt justified in his expectation of an eventful evening.

Lomax, Harvey Clemens and Aubrey Reed arrived together and Ursula Barnes a few minutes later. She was pale and she had dark rings under her eyes to tell of sleepless nights. The black wool frock she wore accentuated her pallor but gave her an air of distinction that was not lost on Dampier. There was really no obvious reason why Richard should shop elsewhere. She spoke to Dampier briefly, acknowledged the others then sat a little apart, making it clear that for her this was no social occasion. Janice moved to sit beside her but got a cold reception. Alfred came at last and Erica brought him upstairs. He had evidently walked in the rain a good deal further than the distance between the two houses. His eyes sought his wife's anxiously. Dampier missed nothing.

He saw his sister standing at the top of the stairs surveying her guests and watched her with the eyes of a stranger. She had the bleached dignity and charm of faded chintz but her face, even her eyes were empty of vitality. He was to blame for that; he was a parasite, draining away her life and she encouraged him. Why? Did she have any regrets? He had no idea. She spoke, raising her voice to gather their attention: 'There's no reason why we shouldn't start playing if that's what everybody wants.'

'Yes, let's start. The suspense of waiting for that terrible man is killing me!' Aubrey Reed, heavily facetious.

Erica smiled, then her gaze fell on Young, lying back in his chair, sleeping it off, and her smile faded. She turned to Lomax. 'All right! Edgar and Janice, I know you both like to go for limit hands so will you make one pair? John and Ursula make another, then I think the rest of us prefer to play as a foursome – Alfred, Harvey, Aubrey and me – is that all right?'

Nobody answered but they moved to their tables,

leaving Young asleep by the stove, his heavy breathing blending with its roar and with the noise of the muted wind. Erica put a shovelful of coke on the fire then joined the others.

Mah-Jongg is not a game for conversation. The rattle of the tiles, an occasional cry in the mysterious language of the initiate, these are the only sounds until a player shouts, 'Mah-Jongg!' Then his tiles are checked, scoring begins and chips pass from hand to hand in settlement of debts. Afterwards the tiles are reshuffled and the walls rebuilt for the next game. It is during this last operation that recriminations may break out but these are rare for Mah-Jongg is not a game for partners, every man is for himself alone.

Dampier found it an odd experience to be playing the game again. In the past he had always been paired with Pussy Welles and between them they had acquired a reputation for phenomenal limit hands and for playing without a word spoken. Even the declaration of Mah-Jongg was made in silence, the player would merely brush his hand over the tiles so that they fell face upwards on the table. Pussy was always absorbed in the play – out to win, which she usually did; she had a card-index memory and a sixth sense for his intentions. He could recall the faint smile on her lips as she made a deft exchange of tiles and placed the new one in its appropriate place. He was finding it disturbingly easy to recall her at any time; unsought and uninvited her image would steal into and take possession of his mind. Sometimes, as now, he saw her in some remembered context of pleasure or relaxation but mostly she appeared as she had been on that last afternoon of her life and he would strive vainly to close his mind to the recollection.

'Mah-Jongg.' Ursula said without the smallest grain of interest. She laid her tiles on the table, the poorest of hands yielding only a meagre score.

He smiled at her, touched by a sudden sympathy. Why should she have to submit to playing this nonsensical game when all her thoughts were concentrated on her husband awaiting trial for murder?

'You're bored and no wonder! You don't have to play.'

She looked at her watch. 'The superintendent hasn't come yet. Do you think they will release Ricky?'

'I'm sure they will.'

At Erica's table, Aubrey Reed was being temperamental, it was obvious that he and Harvey had quarrelled, she knew the signs. Aubrey drummed on the table top with the tips of his manicured nails while Harvey hunched over the tiles, studying them as though he was deciphering an obstinate code. Most of the time she could put up with them for John's sake. He liked to have them round, they amused him, but tonight her nerves were on edge, she sensed trouble and the two of them were an added irritant.

Aubrey tapped viciously on the table with a tile. 'For God's sake, Harvey, hurry up! It's like watching a bad film in slow motion.'

Harvey said nothing but continued to deliberate over his discard, arranging and re-arranging the tiles in his hand. Aubrey turned to Erica conversationally:

'When I was in Singapore the Chinese used to say, "The sound of tiles falling should be as the patter of raindrops in a summer shower." Speed is the essence of the game, don't you agree?'

She would have liked to smack his sallow effeminate face or, at least to say something that would bite into his smug self esteem but she contented herself with silence.

'He read that in the book of instructions,' Harvey said.

'What did you say?' Aubrey demanded, his voice rising.

Harvey raised his eyes and surveyed his adversary mildly. 'I said that you read that bit about the patter of raindrops in the instruction book. You were only forty-eight hours in Singapore, in a transit camp, and I doubt if you saw a Chinaman.'

Aubrey went white. 'What do you know about where I've been and what I've done?' His calm was ominous.

But Harvey was single-minded and determined to elaborate his theme. 'In any case I don't think they have summer showers, more like tropical downpours . . .'

'Will you shut up and play the game?' Aubrey was leaning forward over the table, glaring up into Harvey's bland and rather stupid face.

'It's like a lot of these so called Chinese sayings – made up to sound clever. I've heard that most Chinese play the game with cards and they wouldn't make a noise anyway . . .'

'You bloody fool!' Aubrey hissed. 'My God, why do I put up with him? He nauseates me!'

She should have intervened – poured oil, but she had no intention of doing so. Let the little rats fight if they wanted to. But Mitford was acutely embarrassed, his fair complexion flushed.

'Really!' He shifted uncomfortably in his chair.

Aubrey turned his aggression on him. 'You were going to say?'

'Just that we should get on with the game,' Alfred

said. He might be a lion on the rugby field but he was a coward off it.

She could not help comparing the men she met with her brother and none of them came well out of the comparison. Despite his deformity he was the only real man amongst them; she was proud of him, but her pride blended with a profound pity and recently, with fear.

She was sitting where she could see the whole room. Lomax and Janice Mitford seemed to be absorbed in their game but John and the Barnes girl had given up all pretence of playing, they were deep in conversation. At least, he was talking and she was listening, hanging upon his every word. She found that she resented Ursula Barnes but she could not say why. Perhaps in some self protective illogical fashion she was blaming the girl because they looked like releasing her husband. It had been such a satisfactory solution but now, who knew what might come? John was missing the Welles girl; there could be no doubt about that, and he would continue to miss her until someone else came along. Well, that could be arranged, plenty of girls would be flattered by his attention once they got to know him. Now that she understood that it was essential to him there would be no problem; she had not understood at first. But no more of the intellectual type! She tried to bring her attention back to the game which she had been playing automatically while her thoughts ranged wide. It was useless to think of and plan for the future until she was sure that there would be one. Everything depended on what this policeman found out; what there was for him to find out.

The door bell.

Erica went downstairs to receive him.

Wycliffe came upstairs, blinking in the light and

looking less like a policeman than ever. He was smiling, a little nervous, diffident. He might have been a benevolent don looking in on an undergraduate party. A mouse where they looked for a lion.

He said polite things and Erica led him to a seat on the couch. She offered him a glass of white wine. 'We always do cheese and wine, it's become a tradition. I hope it suits you. You can have red if you prefer it.' The superintendent smiled and nodded, trying not to miss anything. He turned to Ursula Barnes, 'I have some good news for you, Mrs Barnes, I'm sure you won't mind the others hearing it, your husband is likely to be released on Monday; the charge will be withdrawn.'

An involuntary exclamation from Ursula, incredulity and relief. Then a little silence followed by them all congratulating her. Alfred Mitford's pleasure in the news seemed to subside first, he tried to make his remark sound casual, man to man, 'I suppose this means that you start all over again.'

Wycliffe shrugged. 'Not altogether, Mr Mitford, we have quite a lot to go on.'

Dampier tried next. 'Is Barnes being released because of fresh evidence?'

The superintendent seemed to consider the question. 'There has been a certain amount of fresh evidence but it is mainly a matter of our making a new approach. At first this crime was considered in isolation, now we believe that it is linked with others.'

'Others?'

'Another murder and an attempted murder.'

Dampier looked unbelieving. 'And where are these crimes supposed to have happened?'

Wycliffe was casual. 'Oh, in this neighbourhood.'

Reed's irritating high pitched laugh. 'But even in this village murder is unlikely to pass unnoticed.'

'You think so, Mr Reed?' Wycliffe sipped his wine. 'I can assure you that murder is all too likely to pass unnoticed when it is skilfully undertaken.'

Lomax had spoken little, now he intervened as though to make an academic point. 'But surely, superintendent, we are told that the murderer who displays ingenuity is more likely to be caught.'

Wycliffe nodded. 'That is probably true but I think you are confusing ingenuity with skill. One of our victims was pushed over a cliff – that was a very skilful murder but it could hardly be called ingenious. In the absence of an eye-witness there can be no proof against the murderer.'

'Horner!'

'Yes, Mr Dampier, Pussy Welles' husband. I have little doubt that he was murdered.'

'And the attempted murder?'

The superintendent looked at the sleeping Young. 'He was lucky to escape with his life, don't you think? There was no intention that he should. That was an attempt at murder which was ingenious but not skilful. A full investigation at the time would almost certainly have brought the criminal to book.'

'But who . . . ?'

The landlord stirred in his sleep and opened his eyes. He looked round, vaguely at first, then when he realized that he was the centre of attention he became mildly truculent. 'What's all this, then?'

'We were talking about Arthur Horner,' Wycliffe said quickly.

'Pussy's husband.' He blinked sleepily.

'Yes.'

'He fell over the cliff at Clegar – killed himself.' He turned the uninjured aspect of his face to Wycliffe, sufficiently awake now to be self-conscious.

'That's what they said in the papers but do you think he *fell*?'

'He might have jumped for all I know.'

'Or have been pushed?'

The landlord was silent, evidently deciding how to react. He took out a cigarette and lit it, ostentatiously deliberate. 'I suppose you know what you're talking about, superintendent.'

'You should know better – you were there.'

Young faced him and it was strange to see the colour drain from the living side of his face so that it rivalled the other in its pallor. 'What the hell *are* you talking about?' The words were aggressive but their manner was not. He looked round nervously, furtively.

'At the time Horner died the police had no reason to suppose that it was anything but an accident and so their inquiry was superficial. Recently my men have been delving a little deeper and although five years have passed they found a witness ready to swear that you were on the cliff at Clegar that evening at about the time Horner was supposed to have fallen.'

Young puffed at his cigarette, thoughtful, cautious. 'I'm not denying that I was on the cliff that evening.'

'But you didn't volunteer the information at the time.'

The landlord was aggrieved. 'Why should I? There was no call.'

'Not if you had a conversation with Horner shortly before his death?'

'But I didn't! Whoever says that is a liar! Look here! I don't know what you're trying to pin on me but I never spoke to Horner that night nor laid a finger on him!'

Wycliffe spoke in a low voice that hardly carried across the room. 'You may be speaking the truth but in that case you saw someone else talking to him and for some reason you chose to keep quiet about it. You continued to keep quiet when two years later you were almost killed in a car smash that was deliberately contrived. Why?'

Young was a pitiful sight but he spoke firmly. 'You're mad! You make it up as you go along.'

Wycliffe shrugged and returned to his seat. Young sat staring at the stove, the ash on his cigarette lengthened. Dampier lit one of his cheroots; Reed, still sitting at the Mah-Jongg table, tapped irritatingly with his nails on the wood. Erica stood up. 'I'll get some coffee.'

Janice Mitford watched her go and sighed, a sigh that was almost a sob.

'What's the matter?' Ursula, in her relief, felt magnanimous.

'It's all right for you, but I'm scared; scared almost out of my wits.'

Harvey Clemens walked over to the window and parted the curtains. 'The rain has stopped; it's moonlight – lovely!'

Aubrey Reed stopped his niggling. 'Superintendent, is the criminal here tonight?' His manner was childish, bantering.

Wycliffe seemed to take the question seriously. 'I suppose it depends on your point of view.'

'That's a damned queer answer.'

'The fault was in the question.'

Mitford still sat by his table but he had swivelled round to face the others. He looked flushed but he was one of those fair complexioned people who have a perennially high colour and the heat of the room was troubling him. His jumbo ears were bright red and little beads of sweat trickled down his lips. He stared at the fire with unblinking eyes, then he seemed to brace himself to speak. 'What possible motive could anybody have for committing these crimes? If what you say is true, somebody murdered Horner, tried to kill Mike Young and succeeded in killing Pussy. It doesn't make sense, does it?'

'Don't forget that the same person framed Barnes, for framed he certainly was,' Wycliffe said.

Dampier fingered the ends of his beard and looked at Mitford, smiling. 'You might say that we've been lucky – so far.'

'Lucky?'

'Nobody's tried to kill us yet.'

Mitford understood; he eyed his wife nervously but Janice was paying no attention, she was following her own thoughts and she wanted to talk.

'She was a *wicked* woman. I know it sounds absurd but I am still more afraid of her dead, than I am of whoever killed her. She had a way of looking at you . . . as though you were a *thing*.' She shook herself, perhaps to dispel a memory. 'I know the exact moment when she decided to take Alfred away from me. I can't explain it but she had been talking to me – just gossiping, she could make herself very agreeable, then, suddenly, she glanced across at Alfred and back at me – no more than that, but I knew and I remembered.'

Ursula was getting bored, she wanted time to relish her own good news but Janice was gathering momentum.

'Of course, men are fools. She had only to lift her

finger to have any one of them come running – *you* know that.'

Ursula felt compelled to say something. 'By all accounts Mike Young managed to resist her – after his accident.'

Janice nodded. 'That always puzzled me. I think he was afraid of her.'

'Perhaps he is sensitive about his disfigurement.'

Janice laughed unpleasantly. 'Are you joking? He manages well enough with that little slut at the inn. In any case, he and Pussy Welles were two of a kind – vicious!' She took a packet of cigarettes from her handbag and offered one to Ursula who refused. 'I've only taken this up since I found out about them – Alfred and her. You have to do something.'

A silence which Ursula refused to bridge.

Soon Janice began again. 'How that woman . . . !' She lowered her voice. 'When I had proof, I made Alfred tell me everything – every detail. You wouldn't credit what she did!' She eyed Ursula appraisingly. 'Of course you're married and you know what men are like. I mean they're all dirty minded and more than dirty minded if you give them a chance, but a woman . . .' She edged closer so that Ursula was enveloped in the smoke from her cigarette. 'She used to make Alfred strip her, then beat her across the buttocks with a cane! Can you believe it? Isn't it disgusting?'

Ursula had had enough. 'I don't know, it might be rather fun. I must see what Ricky thinks . . .'

Fortunately Erica returned with the coffee and there was a general commotion. Young seemed to rouse himself from a deep reverie, looked at his pocket watch and stood up. 'It's time I was going. I must be back in time to cash up.'

Perfunctory farewells, then Erica went downstairs with him. They heard the front door bang and she came back up, looking relieved. She sat by Ursula. 'A strange man, I feel sorry for him. You'd never think that before his accident he was the most eligible bachelor in the district. What a tragedy! Of course it's not only his disfigurement, it's the drink.'

'He frightens me,' Janice said. 'A violent man.'

'Oh, no!' Erica was just a little too quick, too emphatic. 'Before all this he was the kindest of men, a rough diamond perhaps, but kind and gentle.' She was blushing. 'It was all her fault, none of this would have happened if it hadn't been for her. I'm glad she's gone but it's too late now, somebody should have killed her before she had the chance to sow the seeds of so much wickedness.'

Wycliffe was looking at her with interest. 'That is what she did, Miss Dampier. She sowed the seeds of wickedness.'

Dampier saw the animation in his sister's face and wondered; it was a rare phenomenon. He wished they would all go home, he wanted to think. Wycliffe would get somewhere, that much was obvious but would he recognize the truth when he saw it? Pussy had delighted in weaving complex patterns, she contrived, collected and relished the memory of situations, gloated over them as a connoisseur and achieved what pleasure she knew in planning others. To discover any truth about her it was necessary to break clean through the web of her contrivance. He had reason to be grateful to her for five bearable years but she was a dangerous woman and if ever he had doubts of that, their last afternoon together would have dispelled them.

They were going, thank God! The Mitfords first.

Janice, her voice harsh and brittle, tight-lipped. 'Good-bye, John. Thanks for putting up with me.' Alfred's soft clammy hand. 'Thanks for a pleasant evening, John.'

A pleasant evening!

Lomax hovered uncertainly, then in a moment of decision said, 'I must go,' and went. Reed and Clemens, Ursula Barnes: 'Don't worry about me now, John.' She smiled; suddenly she seemed beautiful.

Wycliffe was cryptic. 'Stir the mixture and allow to stand over night.'

Dampier heard Erica seeing them off. The liturgy of farewell. Then the front door slammed, she shot the bolt and after a moment, came back upstairs. She stood by his side, ruffled his hair. 'You're tired, boy. Time for bed.'

Silver moonlight and a bitter wind off the sea; more like Christmas than Easter. Wycliffe hurried up the lane from the Dampiers', the church clock struck twelve, some of the strokes loud and clear, the sound of others snatched by the wind and scattered over the moor. The square etched in the cold light, deserted, no lights in the houses, none in the windows of the inn. He let himself in very quietly and tip-toed across the lobby to the telephone. Afterwards he went out again and walked up and down the square, smoking his pipe, until he was joined by a young constable. It was nearly one when he finally went indoors leaving the constable to watch until morning.

'What do I do if he comes out, sir?'

'Follow him but let him see you're doing it, then he won't go far.'

'I'm bound to be seen when it gets light.'

'Doesn't matter. Keep an eye on the back and the front doors. When people start moving about you can go home; put in your report at the station.'

He remembered similar nights when the whim of a superior had kept him from a warm bed. 'Are you married?'

'No, sir.'

'That's something then, isn't it?'

Chapter Eight

Wycliffe couldn't sleep; his mind was over active and his stomach was soured by the red wine he drank with his dinner. Easy to get into bad habits away from home. He tumbled and tossed for an hour then switched on the light, got up and turned out the contents of his briefcase, looked for something to focus his attention. Pussy Welles' crosswords, they should be better than counting sheep. He found a ball-point and got back into bed. He picked one at random and it was easier than he had expected; he was not an addict but he could manage this.

Beheld both monarch and mouse, two words, five and three.

'*A cat may look at a king provided she doesn't take him for a mouse?*' The solution was obviously, *Pussy cat*, but he had the quotation wrong.

> *Pussy cat, pussy cat, where have you been?*
> '*I've been to London to see the Great Queen.*'
> *Pussy cat, pussy cat, what saw you there?*
> '*I saw a little mouse under her chair.*'

That was it. Too many damned cats in this case. Try this: *Ruler of all the dim rich city*, six letters. Ah! It was Tennyson who first kindled his love of words. *For all the sacred mount of Camelot and all the dim rich city, roof by roof* . . . Even at two in the morning he could thrill to their music. He wrote in *Arthur*. Getting on nicely. Three or four more and his eyes began to feel heavy; the medicine worked, he switched off the light and fell asleep. He had a muddled dream and at the climax he was in a car being driven furiously by Mike Young along a cliff road when suddenly the road wasn't there, they were falling . . . falling . . . falling . . . He woke, clutching at the bedclothes, certain that he had called out and feeling foolish. It was broad daylight. The pages of Pussy's crosswords were scattered over the floor.

He met Sylvie on the stairs. 'No time for coffee this morning and you'll have to wait for breakfast. He's in bed.'

'What's the matter with him, is he ill?'

She grinned. 'You could say that.'

'Hangover?'

She nodded. 'He must have been at it for a good part of the night.'

'Is he often like that?'

She looked at him, seemed about to say something but changed her mind. 'I must be off else you won't get your breakfast.'

Darley turned up before Wycliffe had finished. 'Coffee?'

'No thanks, I had mine two hours ago.' He had obviously taken umbrage. Soon it came out. 'You had the inn watched last night; I saw the constable's report at the nick.'

'Did he see anything?'

'Not of Young. He kept back and side door under observation all night but according to his report, he saw nobody but Mitford.'

'What was Mitford doing?'

'Standing by his garden gate smoking, for over an hour, between two and three.'

'Turned out by his wife I shouldn't wonder. Did Mitford see our man?'

'Apparently not. Our chap kept in the shadow; he wasn't sure of his brief and he thought he'd better play safe. But he could see Mitford all right, in the moonlight.'

'Did he have him under observation the whole time?'

'Not quite. He didn't actually see him go indoors – one minute he was there and the next he was gone. You know what it is, keeping observation on a man a hundred and fifty yards off in the moonlight. The eyes play tricks. Why? What's it all about, sir?'

'Just a hunch that didn't come off,' Wycliffe said. 'I'm glad I'm not married to that woman.'

'I'm glad I'm not married to any woman,' Darley growled.

'Then you'd better come with me, I'm going to talk to Aubrey Reed and his friend.'

Inspector Darley was not amused and the super-intendent went alone.

Even years of police work and a tolerant disposition had never reconciled him to queers and this worried him for he half believed that what we hate most in others is what we fear in ourselves. He consoled himself with the thought that never since puberty had he turned his eyes from a pretty girl.

Reed answered the door, wearing jeans and a polo necked jersey. He seemed a little resentful, rather more, apprehensive. Wycliffe was taken into the sitting-room, a large room with nineteen-twentyish furniture; two overblown settees upholstered in brocade and armchairs to match; a china cabinet with some nice pieces, a screen with tapestry panels, two or three poufs and a couple of standard lamps. The only pictures were four Beardsley drawings and Burne Jones which could have been a reproduction, over the mantelpiece. Heavy curtains, partly drawn across the windows shut out the sunlight and although there was a fire in the grate, the room had an unused feel, it was like the period rooms one sees in museums, selfconscious and depressing. Wycliffe had to sit in an armchair which was like being trapped in the embrace of a feather bed, but Reed sat himself on one of the little stools by the fire and jabbed at the coals with a brass poker. His figure was boyish but his face had long since lost all trace of the mobility of youth, the lines were set and deepening. Thirty-two or three.

Wycliffe took his time. Reed lit a cigarette and ignored him. If it was a game to see who would speak first, it was never played out for Harvey Clemens opened the door and stood, looking surprised and uncertain on the threshold. He wore a blue and white apron and clutched a tea-towel. He muttered something and would have gone but Wycliffe stopped him. Reed snapped:

'If you're coming in, for God's sake take off that ridiculous apron; you look like a butcher boy!'

Whatever had inspired and sustained his rebellious mood of the night before, Harvey was submissive now; he took off his apron and rolled it up with the tea-towel. 'I was washing up, I didn't know there was anybody here.' He perched on the edge of a chair and looked round, apprehensive but determined to be affable. He had left the door ajar and a Siamese walked in, inspected the other occupants of the room and jumped on to Harvey's lap, flexing its claws through the jeans

144

so that he winced. Reed eyed him with disdain.

'I told you yesterday evening that Dr Barnes is to be released tomorrow.'

'Does that mean that you are back where you started or do you have someone else in mind?' Reed was jaunty, ironic.

'It means that despite Dr Barnes' foolish behaviour, we are satisfied that he did not kill Miss Welles. We still have to find out who did.'

'She deserved it anyway, didn't she, Abel?' Clemens spoke to the cat.

'It must have been one of her men friends.' Half a statement, half a question from Reed.

'Did you count yourself as one of those, Mr Reed?'

Aubrey made a sinuous movement of the shoulders, wholly feminine. 'Of course not!'

'What about you, Mr Clemens?'

'I hated her, she was a bitch!' He fondled the cat on his lap. 'Among other things, she tried to poison Abélard, didn't she, old boy?'

'Don't be a bigger fool than God made you,' Reed snapped. 'She didn't poison the cat!'

Clemens looked injured. 'The vet said he'd been poisoned and you said . . .'

'Never mind what I said, it was intended as a joke. In any case, the superintendent doesn't want to listen to gossip.'

Wycliffe toook a sheaf of typewritten papers from his briefcase and turned the pages. 'We have to consider every possibility,' he said, without obvious relevance. 'How long have you lived in Kergwyns, Mr Reed?'

Reed looked surprised. 'Oh, eight or nine years.' He considered. 'Yes, we came here, bought this place and set up in business nine years ago.'

Wycliffe stroked the side of his face with his finger-tips and mused over his papers. 'I know very little about the antique trade but surely this was a very odd place to choose?'

'You think so? You can set up an antique business anywhere, once you have a connection.'

It was Clemens who answered the unspoken question. 'We had a good start. My father had a business in Bristol on quite a big scale. When he died, we sold up and came down here.'

'We?'

'Aubrey and me. Aubrey worked for my father as a buyer going round to sales, that sort of thing.'

Wycliffe nodded. So that was it! 'And you, what did you do in your father's business, Mr Clemens?'

Clemens wriggled like a guilty schoolboy. 'I didn't have much to do with the business.'

'So it was your capital and Mr Reed's experience?'

'I can't see what all this has to do with you, super-intendent!' Reed was petulant.

'Background, Mr Reed, just background. In any case, there's nothing dishonourable in a partnership between capital and experience, is there?'

However they interpreted the rhetorical question, both Reed and his partner seemed to find it disquieting. Wycliffe turned over the pages of his document.

'In your statement to Inspector Darley, you said that you had known Miss Welles only since she came to Kergwyns to live.'

'Well?'

'I want to know if that is strictly true. It appears that she was in the habit of spending her holidays in St Ives before she came down here to live and that she used to visit Kergwyns in company with Mr Young at the inn.

This is a small village and you may have heard or seen something of her.' Wycliffe left the invitation vague, unspecific. 'We want to know everything there is to know about her life both before and after she settled here.' He saw them exchange looks but seemed not to notice.

'We knew her by sight, of course,' Reed admitted.

'And by reputation,' Harvey added.

'A bit wild,' Wycliffe suggested.

'Mike Young was the centre of a lively set in those days, most of them a good deal younger than he was. She was with them.' It was obvious that Reed wanted to appear cooperative without giving anything away.

'Nude bathing parties at night – that sort of thing,' Harvey said and earned a black look.

'A few youngsters out for mischief,' Reed was tolerantly contemptuous.

'Anyone who lives in the village now? – apart from yourselves that is.'

Harvey was dying to tell the story, he was a born scandal-monger. 'Alfie Mitford was one of them but they were mostly strangers – visitors.'

'But there was more to these parties than just bathing without costumes,' the superintendent prompted.

Reed shrugged. 'There was a certain amount of pairing off, you don't want us to draw a diagram, do you?'

'And fights,' Clemens put in. He was excited, like a child with a story to tell.

'Fights?'

'She used to take flashlight photographs.'

'Who did?'

'Why, Pussy Welles. She used to organize everything.'

'Look here, superintendent, there's no point in raking all this up. It was years ago and we were all a lot younger and a lot sillier. It's best forgotten.' Reed's squeaky voice was almost pleading.

Wycliffe eyed him with distaste. 'I shall be glad to forget it, Mr Reed, once I am satisfied that it has nothing to do with my case. Until then, I expect you to answer my questions. About these fights . . .'

'It was really all-in wrestling,' Clemens said, 'like you see on the television. I fought Mike Young three times and beat him every time. You wouldn't think so would you? I'm a lot stronger than I look, aren't I, Aubrey?'

'And while you were wrestling, Pussy Welles took photographs?'

'Oh, yes, she used to photograph everything.' He needed no more encouragement and Reed was powerless to stop him. With the enthusiasm of a boy recounting his favourite story he told his tale of vicious sensualism incited and directed – stage managed – by the dead girl.

She couldn't have been more than nineteen!

'She was certainly an unusual young woman. Did she try to use any of these photographs?'

Clemens was suddenly canny, he looked slyly at Reed. Aubrey was scornful. 'There's no point in holding back now, you fool! Of course she used them – after she came to live at Kergwyns. Where do you think her furniture came from? Every piece in that cottage is rightfully mine. She used to give me instructions like a wealthy client – money no object. But she wasn't satisfied with that. When she had all the furniture she wanted, she started trying to get cash.' He stood up and took a cigarette from a box on the mantelshelf, lit it and leaned nonchalantly with his elbow on the shelf. 'I drew the line at that.'

Wycliffe heaved himself out of the armchair and walked to the window, perhaps to remind himself that the sun was shining outside. 'How?'

'I told her she could do what she liked with the photographs.' He warmed to his role now that there was no purpose in concealment.

'And how do you explain this sudden access of courage?' Wycliffe threw the question over his shoulder without bothering to turn round.

'I had the sense to stop and think. Until then I did what she wanted without stopping to make a rational appraisal of her hold over me – a mistake made by many victims of blackmail, I imagine.' (He was right there!) 'What could she do? She could send copies of the photographs to a few of my friends, shock one or two of my customers. She might even try to involve me with your people but the photographs were five years old and I was prepared to take a chance.' He preened himself.

'What happened when you refused to pay?' Wycliffe still had his back to the room.

'Once she understood that I meant it, she took it very well. She laughed. "Photographs? There aren't any, I destroyed them years ago." So you see, superintendent, I – we, had no reason to harm her.'

The smirk on his lips as he sat down left no doubt that he believed himself well out of a tricky situation.

'But she might have blackmailed others – not so strong-minded.' The superintendent was scathing.

'Alfie Mitford, for instance,' Clemens said.

'Shut up, you fool!' Reed's voice was almost a shriek.

'Why shouldn't I tell him? She came here the day she was murdered . . .'

Reed sprang at him like a cat, clawing at his face. 'I'll kill you! I'll kill you!' But Clemens stood up, lifting Reed with him like a baby, and catching his arms he pinioned them and Reed yelped.

Clemens released him. 'I didn't mean to hurt you.' Reed collapsed on to the settee, shaking with temper and sobbing. Clemens stood over him, his great moon-face creased with concern. 'He's easily upset, you can never tell . . .'

'I'll leave you to console him,' Wycliffe said.

'But don't you want to know what she said?'

'Well?'

'She didn't usually come here but she came Thursday morning and after talking for a bit she asked if we'd heard any rumours. She said it was going around that Mike Young's accident wasn't an accident at all but that somebody tried to kill him. Aubrey wouldn't say anything, he's good at playing it cool, he just said why did people want to bring that up after all this time? She said it didn't matter but perhaps somebody ought to ask Alfie Mitford where the oil came from.'

'Where the oil came from?'

'Yes; ask Alfie Mitford that.'

'Is that all?'

Clemens was crestfallen. Wycliffe let himself out, slamming the front door so that it rattled. 'Bloody little rats!'

He had forgotten that it was Sunday – Easter Sunday – but the square reminded him, it was more lively than he had yet seen it, people coming out of church and gossiping in the sunshine. Women in new hats, several of the men in sober suits and well brushed bowlers.

Erica Dampier looking more bleached than ever in a beige two-piece, talked earnestly to the vicar. Janice Mitford, alone, looking haggard, she seemed on the point of coming over to him but changed her mind. Even the dogs were having a day out, sniffing at this and that and at each other.

A film set, Wycliffe thought, would be more convincing.

The bar was crowded, Sylvie and a little rat faced man with a dangling cigarette, coped as best they could but Sylvie caught the superintendent's eye and with a gesture as plain as words told him, 'He's still in bed.'

Lunch was late and served by a harassed elderly woman who mixed up the orders. Evidently there was disorganization behind the scenes and the food was cold. Not that Wycliffe was critical, he ate mechanically and brooded.

Barnes had been fixed by the dead girl; now he was inclined to wonder whether she had not played the game another move ahead. Had she foreseen that the case against Barnes would come unstuck and provided another candidate in Alfie Mitford? Bloody ridiculous! And yet he was being led by the nose to interest himself in Mitford; first the photograph with the newspaper cuttings concealed in the frame, then this devious procedure to set Clemens gossiping. What other motive could she have had? 'Somebody should ask Alfie Mitford where the oil came from.' Presumably the oil that caused Young's smash. Mitford had been an amateur racing enthusiast and the picture showed him with his car. Was the whole thing too silly or was it what he might expect from the twisted mind of the author of *God and Maggie Jones*? He groaned and a visitor at the next table looked across sympathetically. 'Not very good is it? The meat's like leather.'

Why couldn't it have been a nice straightforward case with a jealous lover waiting to say 'Yes, I did it and I'd do it again'? If he was right and he was still dancing to Pussy's tune, then she had wanted him to take Mike Young's smash into account. He had to bear in mind the possibility that Mitford really was the culprit. He toyed absently with a couple of tinned peaches swimming in a milky gravy.

Chapter Nine

For Ursula Barnes Sunday morning was an anti-climax. After the strain she seemed to have entered a limbo of the emotions which denied her even a sense of relief. Instead of the excitement of anticipation, instead of pleasure or even satisfaction she experienced only a numbing emptiness, an intolerable detachment. Most of the time her throat felt constricted and she was on the brink of tears. She had the sense to know that it would come right when Ricky was back but she had to get through this endless day. She forced herself to do the cottage chores, trying to believe that she was getting it ready for him but it was unreal. What if something went wrong and they didn't let him go? She cooked a meal which she hardly touched. She told herself that within twenty-four hours he would be sitting opposite her again and tried, desperately, to see him in the eye of her mind but all she achieved was an anonymous blur. It was the last straw and the intolerable tension dissolved into a paroxysm of weeping.

Then she felt better. She washed her face in cold water and decided to go for a walk. She followed the path by the stream towards the cove but when it reached the rocky defile above the beach she chose instead the cliff path and climbed to a grassy promontory and sat there. A quiet spring afternoon, the sea shining like silver in the sun, the air sweet and balmy, the gorse full blown in flower and bumble bees stocking up for their broods. The old recipe trotted out every year but always a best buy.

She began to relax; she had a lichen covered boulder at her back and the turf was springy. She watched midget waves breaking in a lace of foam, a dog pursuing an uncertain scent along the crumbling bank of the stream, gulls swooping and quarrelling over something on the flat rocks at the other side of the cove. She felt drowsy and perhaps she dozed for she was startled by heavy foot-falls that seemed close, a man hurrying along the cliff path towards her. He was tall, heavily built and he wore a navy track suit.

'Alfred!'

'Ursula!'

He was out of breath and seemed embarrassed. She hoped that after saying polite things he would go away but he didn't, he loomed over her and fumbled for words. 'Getting some exercise; since I've given up actually playing games I find it difficult to keep my weight down. I do a lot of reffing of course but it's not the same.' This came in disjointed phrases with long pauses in between.

'No, I suppose not,' Ursula said when it seemed certain that no more would come.

'Do you mind if I sit down? Just for a moment?' He sat beside her, his arms round his knees and stared out to sea. 'Janice and I were delighted to hear about Ricky. You must be relieved.' He didn't sound delighted.

'Yes.'

'It's really odd why that superintendent hasn't been to see me, I thought he was interviewing everybody . . . everybody in any way connected with Pussy Welles.'

154

He spoke her name as though it was an indelicacy which had to be got over. 'The inspector took a statement from me in the beginning but that was all. I suppose I ought to be glad – I mean glad that they are not interested in me but now I'm a bit worried if they are going to start all over again.'

Ursula had little sympathy or patience with men who, like infants, want to be kissed and made better, and she resented the implication that everything was all right as long as Ricky was the scapegoat. So she gave him no encouragement but he blundered on.

'A school teacher is especially vulnerable to ill-natured gossip and Janice is very . . . To be quite frank, I only told the inspector part of the truth . . .'

'You can soon put that right.'

But he was not to be snubbed. 'You see, I knew Pussy before she came to Kergwyns to live. She used to come here for her holidays.'

Bit by bit the story came out punctuated by excuses, apologies, explanations. She heard about the nude bathing, about the fights on the beach, about the photographs and most of all about his infatuation for Pussy Welles which he seemed to regard as a disease for which he deserved pity rather than blame. 'I was very young and irresponsible.' (He must have been in his early or middle twenties.) 'I had a difficult childhood; my parents were over protective.' (All parents are either over protective or indifferent.) 'The gradual initiation into sex which most youngsters manage in their teens was telescoped for me into a few weeks, years late.' Once he had stopped and looked at her with concern, 'I hope I'm not shocking you.'

'No, you're not shocking me,' Ursula said. But he was though not in the way that he feared.

'I was a young teacher at the same school as now and terrified that all this might get out – it would have finished me.' He picked at the loose threads of his trousers and collected his thoughts to begin again.

Ursula watched the sky and sea, sometimes she would follow the flight of a bird or shift her position to sit more comfortably. He was puzzled by her detachment; how could she be so indifferent to his confidences?

'Then I met Janice at a conference and after a short engagement we were married. The next I heard of Pussy Welles, she was married too and although she had come to live at St Ives, I thought that she would be as anxious to forget the past as I was. For a time it seemed that I was right, then her husband was killed and she took that cottage of Mike Young's. I mean, why did she have to come to live in the village?'

With a naive egoism he told how Pussy Welles established herself in the village. He tried to keep out of her way at first but Janice involved him in the social life of the place so that they were bound to meet and in the end he was paying her clandestine visits. 'It wouldn't be true to say I didn't want to.' He was blushing like a schoolboy. 'I mean Pussy Welles was a very attractive girl – not only physically . . . and she couldn't be shocked. You never felt *dirty*.' He said the word then winced as though he had been hurt. 'But she was hard! There was no sentiment, no affection, no love. I think she was incapable of love.'

Ursula was learning a lot about men which might be good for Richard.

'Of course, I knew that I was doing wrong – deceiving my wife and so on. I also knew that I was bound to be found out eventually, so I decided to explain to Pussy and to stop seeing her. But when I told her, she looked strange and said, "I was going through a box of junk the other day – you know the sort of thing – stuff I hadn't looked at for years, and I came across some old photographs. You remember the nights we used to go bathing?" I knew what she meant, she didn't need to threaten.'

When he arrived he had been hot from exertion, beads of sweat on his brow and running down his cheeks, great damp patches under the arms of his track suit; now he shivered. 'It was horrible after that – I mean being *made* to do the most intimate things . . . She used to put me through what she called *love tests* – I got to hate her! Then Janice found out and I had to stop going there. In a way I was relieved but it didn't really solve anything because she still had the photographs and she could still ruin my career any time she felt so inclined.'

'But she didn't.'

Mitford shook his head. 'She really didn't have much chance, it wasn't long after Janice found out that she was killed.'

Ursula was mystified. Why should he be so anxious to establish that he had a motive for the crime? Was this a preamble to confession? For a moment she felt uneasy. Was it so unlikely that a murderer should confess his crime, explain it, justify it, then kill his confidante? She shivered. To be washed up on the shore one fine morning.

'You're cold! How utterly thoughtless of me to keep you here like this!'

Then she felt a fool. 'No, I'm not cold, not a bit.' To punish herself she added: 'I suppose you realize that what you've told me is an admission that you had a strong motive for killing her?'

He sat, shoulders drooping, scuffling the ground with his feet. 'I know.'

'Then why tell me?'

'Because I've got to talk to somebody and I can't talk to Janice.' He was silent for a long time, then he burst out, 'And you haven't heard everything yet, there was the business with the oil . . .'

'The *oil?*'

'Pussy came to my house on the afternoon of the day she died; she hadn't been there for months. Luckily, Janice was in the back garden. She talked for a few minutes then she said, "If anything happens, Alfie, I should tell them about the oil. If you don't they'll get to know just the same, then it would look bad for you." ' He shuddered. 'She was a devil! – I asked her what was likely to happen and she just laughed, then Janice came in and she went.'

'But what's all this about oil?' Ursula was losing patience.

He spoke so quietly that it was difficult to hear. 'The oil that made Mike Young skid came from my garage, a five gallon drum I used for waste from the sump. It was in the days when I used to do rally driving.'

'Did you put the oil on the road?'

'Oh, God, no!'

'But the drum of oil came from your garage. Stolen?'

He nodded.

'Which gives a strong presumption that Young's crash was no accident but an attempt to kill him – just as the superintendent said last night.'

Mitford writhed. 'He knows. I'm sure he knows, just like she said he would. And it makes me an accessory.'

'Why didn't you report the loss of the oil at the time?'

'Pussy advised me not to get involved.'

'You told her?'

He nodded. 'What shall I do?'

Ursula was angry but she realized that it was useless to tell him what she thought. 'I don't know what you should do but I'll tell you this much, if Ricky had told the police the truth he wouldn't be in prison now.'

Mitford waited but when he saw that there was no more to come, he got up. 'I'll think it over. It was good of you to listen . . . You won't say anything?'

'I won't say anything.'

'Thanks. You're a good sport.'

Christ, I hope not! Ursula was learning fast. She watched him loping away down the path to the valley then she got up herself and set off in the opposite direction.

She had walked some distance along the cliff path before she thought of where she was going. She couldn't face a return to her solitary vigil at the cottage so she decided to continue along the cliffs to the village and to call on the Dampiers or to have tea at the pub. For once she needed to be among people. She reached the ruins of a mine engine house with a truncated stack perched on the cliff edge and from the ruin a grassy track ran in the direction of Kergwyns church tower. It occurred to her that this might be a short cut to the village and she decided to follow it. As she moved away from the sea the sense of desolation increased and soon the broad track petered out into a maze of rutted paths among the heather but she could see the tower straight ahead and there seemed no reason why she should not reach it. Overhead a buzzard lazily quartered the ground but otherwise there was no sign of life.

As she approached the village she had to cross a couple of tiny fields bounded by low walls of huge granite boulders but then she came up against a higher wall of properly mortared stones that she could not possibly climb. It was infuriating, the church tower was less than a hundred yards away, but to her left the wall ended in a marsh with standing water and to her right it seemed to lose itself in a bramble thicket of indeterminate extent and quite impenetrable. She swore with vigour and realized that her behaviour was almost hysterical. 'What the hell is wrong with me? I've just got to go round; it's a nuisance but what of it?'

It was quiet, so quiet that she could hear her heart beating. She set out along the wall and just before the brambles started she came to a little door set in the wall and surmounted by a pointed arch which gave it an ecclesiastical air. If she could open it and if it led into the churchyard, all would be well. It opened easily enough but not into the churchyard. She found herself in the cobbled yard of a farmhouse with outbuildings on two sides and the house on a third. A white painted farm gate separated the yard from a gravelled drive that must lead to the village. There was no sign of life in the house, the windows looked blind and she had only to cross the yard. Just then a little animal scuttled across almost at her feet and disappeared behind a pile of logs. A rat? She hadn't seen it clearly. Then she saw another. In the centre of the cobbled yard there was a Cornish Cross and seated on the plinth, a little brown, stub-tailed creature nibbled at one paw. A lemming! Then she knew where she was. She walked over to the cross and found two more on the plinth at the other side and yet another crouched between the cobbles a yard away; the place was alive with them. The wicket in the big double doors of the outhouse was open and she watched another put its little snub nose out into the sunlight then beat a hasty retreat. She walked over to the shed. When her eyes had adapted to the light she could see the bank of cages with all their doors open and there were lemmings all over the floor. Some were scurrying about, others were crouched, panting and glassy eyed, more lay on their sides, eyes closed, apparently dead.

She hurried out of the shed, closed the door and crossed to the house. As she pressed the bell the door itself yielded, opening into a square hall with stairs on one side, the open door of the kitchen on the other and a glass door with multi-coloured panes straight ahead. Lying in the rainbow pattern of light from the coloured glass, on the floor of the hall, a black and white cat, stretched out in death. For the first time since she entered the courtyard she felt afraid.

'Mr Lomax!' Her voice sounded absurdly tremulous and faint. She tried again. 'Mr Lomax!' This time it was almost a scream but nobody answered. 'Is there anybody in the house?' She hardly knew what to do. Caution and common sense counselled that she should go for help but she hated to go with half a story. She looked into the kitchen, it was empty, a pile of dirty dishes on the draining board, a stove crepitating gently, a couple of tea towels on the rack. On the floor a congealed mess testified to the illness of the cat. She opened the glass door having to step over the cat's body to do it, and found herself in Lomax's study. Lomax was there too, seated at his table, the sunlight streaming down on his greying head. He seemed to be asleep, his head resting on his left arm, but he was dead, shot through the temple. She stood looking down at him feeling quite calm and no longer afraid. She wondered how long he had been dead. Could the killer still be in the house? She strained her ears; nothing but the majestic ticking of the grandfather clock. Then she noticed the gun, lying on the carpet by the chair, just a few inches from the trailing fingers of his right hand. Suicide! The church clock chimed a quarter past three and startled her by its nearness.

There was nothing she could do. She crept out of the room, stepped over the cat and left the glass door ajar. The flowered porcelain knob must already carry one set of her prints. Not that it mattered, she supposed. She reached the yard and then she ran, sending the lemmings scuttling for cover. The drive brought her into the lane just a few yards from the square. She forced herself to walk and to breathe deeply. The square was deserted except for the old men on their seat and a solitary herring gull perched on top of the war memorial like a weather cock.

Lomax was dead. He had shot himself. Did this mean that he was guilty?

At the inn she was lucky to catch both the superintendent and the inspector. She told her story sounding more composed than she felt.

'You go along. I'll telephone the boys and join you later.'

When Darley had gone Wycliffe said, 'Are you all right? . . . Sure? . . . Good girl! This must be the last straw for you.' He sounded genuinely concerned and she hoped she didn't look like a plucky little woman.

Lomax was dead so Lomax could wait. The superintendent went through to the back premises of the inn and up the private stairs. On the landing he hesitated then turned right and threw open the first door. In the room the curtains were drawn and the air was heavy with the smell of stale spirits. Mike Young lay on the bed fully dressed except for his jacket and shoes, snoring in a drunken sleep. An empty whisky bottle lay on the floor.

Wycliffe swept back the curtains and slammed down the window, letting in the sunlight and a breath of air but the only effect on Young was a brief interruption in the rhythm of his breathing. Wycliffe stood over him. 'Even if I succeed in waking him he'll be too drunk to talk!' He put his head into the passage and bellowed: 'Sylvie!' His voice must have been heard half across the square.

But Sylvie was already coming down the passage, pulling a dressing-gown round her. 'What's going on? I was getting ready to go out. Is he gone round the bend?'

She stood in the doorway of the bedroom watching the superintendent with more interest than surprise. The main item of furniture in the room was a chest of drawers, the veneer chipping off, its surface greasy with the grime of years. Wycliffe had yanked out one of the small top drawers and was throwing its contents on to the floor. Handkerchiefs, socks, clean and dirty, ties, loose collars and a few paper backed novels.

'When did you see him last?'

She walked into the room, stepping over the debris. Wycliffe was through with one drawer and starting on the next.

'Just before lunch. I came up to ask him if he wanted anything.'

'And did he?'

She grimaced like a little girl. 'He was just like now. Why? What's he done?'

'I'll ask the questions! What time did he get in last night?'

She had to think. 'Just after closing time – half after ten. He cashed up.'

'Then?'

'I went to bed.'

'Where do you sleep?'

'The room at the head of the stairs. If you want to know, I heard him come up about a quarter past eleven.'

'But he could have gone out again at any time during the night without you knowing?' Wycliffe was busy now with one of the long drawers and the pile of clothing on the floor grew.

'He could have but he didn't.'

'How do you know?' The superintendent stopped what he was doing to give her his undivided attention.

She shrugged. 'Do you want me to tell you what happened or don't you? He did go out and I heard him. Just after two. He'd been moving about in here, keeping me awake, then I heard him pass my door and go downstairs. After a minute or two he opened the back door – the bolt makes a noise.'

'Did you hear him come back?'

'No. I never saw or heard any more of him until just after eight this morning. I looked in here and he was just like you see him now.'

'You mean he's been sleeping it off since then?'

She grinned. 'The bottle was only half empty then.'

'Have you ever seen a gun among his belongings?'

'A gun! What's he supposed to have done, then?'

Wycliffe repeated his question. She tossed her head, clearing the straggling brown hair from her eyes. 'I've never seen him with a gun and I'm never allowed in here. He always locks the door when he goes out and I'm not even allowed to clean it – *as* you can see for yourself.'

'But you told me . . .'

'That I sleep with him. I do sometimes but he always comes to me.'

Wycliffe had reached the bottom of the second long drawer and came up with a battered briefcase. It was locked but he opened it with a safety pin. A few papers. He spread them on top of the chest of drawers. Two birth certificates, a will and a photograph. The first certificate recorded the birth of Charles Michael Holst and the other that of Anna Patricia Holst, eight years later.

'They were brother and sister!' Sylvie looked at the man on the bed in astonishment. For once, something had surprised her. She turned to the superintendent, 'You knew?'

'No, I wondered. They were alike.'

'*Alike!*'

Wycliffe picked up the photograph, a snapshot taken on the pavement outside a dreary looking terraced house, a youngish woman with a baby in her arms and a little boy standing at her side. On the back someone had written in a feminine hand, *Michael 8. Anna 3 months.*

'It looks as though papa's music didn't pay very well.'

Wycliffe collected the papers and put them back, relocking the case. Young snorted vigorously in his sleep and turned over on his side. A man's voice downstairs called, 'Anybody about?'

'See who it is.'

Sylvie went out but came back almost at once with a uniformed constable who looked as though he had just come out of training school. He stared at the cluttered floor and at the man on the bed.

'Well?'

'Inspector Darley would be grateful if you would join him at the house, sir.'

Wycliffe nodded. 'You'll be all right?'

Her smile was contemptuous. 'Is it all right to tidy up?'

He was about to say something, changed his mind, shrugged and went out. The constable followed him.

Chapter Ten

The church clock chimed then struck five. In the courtyard of Lomax's house you could hear the mechanical throat clearing that preceded each stroke and the dissonant overtones that followed. Wycliffe sat on the plinth of the Cornish Cross, morose, introspective. The place was alive with policemen, a car and a van were parked in the courtyard and there was another car in the lane. Half the village seemed to have turned out to watch. A constable at the gate stopped them from coming in but they were out in the lane and some had climbed onto the hedges to get a better view. Not that they could see much; only the comings and goings and the superintendent sitting there.

Now and then a lemming flitted across the cobbles to disappear into the shed and the dead ones were still there.

'They're ready to move the body, sir.' Wycliffe merely growled, but after a while he knocked out his pipe, got up and went indoors.

'Something's happening!' The watchers could hardly be expected to know that the principal in their drama felt redundant, that all the real work was being done without his help or intervention.

Darley had established his headquarters in the kitchen.

'Any idea of when it happened yet?'

Darley smoothed his bald head. 'The doctor says he's been dead for at least fourteen and probably sixteen hours or more. Say, between eleven last night and three this morning with a preference for the earlier time. Slade may be able to give us a better idea when he gets hold of the body.' Darley hesitated, looked down at the papers in front of him, then went on, 'Are we to continue to treat this as murder? That's the first question that has to be answered.'

'Or?'

Darley frowned. 'Suicide, of course.'

'And what do you think?'

'There's no doubt in my mind that he killed himself.'

'Why?

Darley resented being forced to spell it out. 'It seems to me that there's only one explanation of his suicide – guilt.'

'So it's all tied up and we're wasting our time – is that what you're saying? You may be right, but let's get this straight! It's almost certain that already in this case, murder and attempted murder have been passed over as accident. Certainly an innocent man has been arrested. I don't intend to repeat those mistakes. We'll treat this as suicide only when there is no possibility that it could have been murder.'

Darley reddened but said nothing.

'Now, is there anything, so far, in the slightest degree inconsistent with it being suicide?'

Darley nodded towards the stove. 'There's that. It's still alight, which means that it must have been refuelled say, after eleven last night. I understand that they are designed to go for twenty to twenty-four hours once they're fully banked up, and there's still several hours burning left in the fuel bed. I know it seems unlikely that a chap would bank up his fire before shooting himself but you and I know they do some queer things.'

'Any heating in the room where he was?'

'A night storage heater and a coal fire which had gone out.'

'What about the animals? – the cat and the lemmings.'

'You mean the fact that they were poisoned?'

Wycliffe nodded.

'I don't see that kind of behaviour as inconsistent with suicide. Quite the reverse. If the animals were important to him he might well feel that he must take them with him, so to speak.'

'By poison?'

'That might seem the only way open to a man of a sensitive nature.'

'A very good point,' Wycliffe admitted.

In the big front room Lomax had been photographed from every possible angle, seated in his chair, his papers on the desk in front of him but these photographs would never appear in *Nature* nor was it likely that anyone would write his biography. Whatever notoriety he achieved now would spring from his connection with a series of crimes, either as a victim or as their perpetrator.

The technical people had taken over and until they were through, Darley and the superintendent were in the way. A detective held the revolver, suspended by its trigger guard and examined it carefully. 'Two chambers fired, sir.'

'*Two?*' Wycliffe was startled.

'No doubt of it, sir.'

'OK to shift him now, sir?'

Other men lifted the body in which *rigor* had so far advanced that they were forced to lay him on his side on the stretcher. Despite the gaping hole in his temple, his features were composed and only a little paler than in life. They covered him with a sheet and whisked him away to the van outside. For once, the watchers had something to watch.

'There he goes, poor chap!' A middle-aged woman with a large bosom and a soft heart.

'You don't want to waste your sympathy on the likes of him. They say he shot himself because he killed the girl.' An old man with a military moustache who had once been an RSM. 'No room for murderers, hang 'em I say.'

'Well, if he did kill her, she had it coming to her,' the woman retorted.

Back in the house they found the second bullet. It had entered the spine of a book at the end of the room, penetrated through the pages and bedded itself in the plaster. Darley held the mutilated book in his hands, *Eysenck's Handbook of Abnormal Psychology*. 'If he committed suicide, this must be the first, not the second bullet.'

'What?' Wycliffe seemed worried and vague. 'Oh yes, of course, but why did he fire it before turning the gun on himself?'

'I've heard that suicides – genuine ones who really mean to go through with it, have a horror that it won't work. Lomax wanted to make sure that the gun was in working order, he probably hadn't fired the thing for years – if ever.'

'But is it his gun?'

'Oh, yes. It's registered in his name all right. You're not suggesting, sir, that he was firing at someone else?'

Wycliffe shrugged. 'No.'

The fingerprint men were busy with drawers and

cupboard doors. Wycliffe watched them; his manner was apologetic. 'Once you start a murder routine you have to go through with it.'

As each piece of furniture was fingerprinted two other detectives began a meticulous search. If they came across anything of the slightest interest it was put on the desk to be examined by Darley. Wycliffe took up a position by the desk and watched, idly, as the heterogeneous collection increased.

'I suppose you will get them to do a paraffin test on his hands?'

Darley nodded.

'Both hands?'

'Both? No. The gun was found within reach of his right hand. What would be the point of testing the other?'

'I don't know, but have it done.'

The church bell began tolling for evening service, a monotonous clang on the tenor bell. Evidently somebody had decided that the usual cheerful cascade of sound would be inappropriate. There wouldn't be many in the congregation anyway. Wycliffe looked out of the window; the church tower was silhouetted against a brilliant sky, blue with white wisps of cloud turning gold at the edges.

'I'll take a look upstairs.'

'Help yourself.' Darley was preoccupied and glad to see him go.

Wycliffe went out into the passage and up the stairs; stairs and landing were carpeted from wall to wall in plain blue. There were four doors, three bedrooms and one that had been converted to bathroom and lavatory. One of the bedrooms was a lumber room and of the other two, one was a very comfortable looking guest room. Lomax's bedroom was plain and bare by comparison, white walls with no pictures, the floor varnished boards with only a couple of thin mats. The furniture was massive, a mahogany chest of drawers with a mirror over it, a Victorian wardrobe and an armchair upholstered in black leather. But it was the bed that caught attention, a brass bed, the ancestor of them all, gleaming and splendid, complete with patchwork quilt and valances of white damask with lace insertion. Straight out of grandmother's room, a distaff heirloom in which, no doubt, Lomax's mother had been conceived and born. On the wall by the bed, a hanging bookcase crammed with novels, novels of adventure and romance, Scott, Stevenson, Dumas, Hardy, Buchan . . . all tattered through endless re-reading. So Lomax commuted between two worlds of fantasy, one, the world of the great scientist, the other, that of the great adventurer.

And he had tangled with Pussy Welles in the hope that she would give substance to his dreams. Wycliffe wondered how complete and utter disillusionment might subvert such a man. Would it render him capable of killing his Guinevere and viciously displaying her secret flaw? It was certainly possible; in such straits the flesh and blood romantic may not confine his tilting to the windmills. But while his dream world was still intact, could he then, plot with her to kill? Could Lomax have killed Arthur Horner and contrived the crash which almost killed Young? It seemed less likely though not incredible if the besotted man could persuade himself or be persuaded that he was serving his love. Even *Dickson McCunn* fought a bloody battle in defence of his private ideal of chivalry.

On the chest of drawers there were three photographs

in oval silver frames, one of Lomax himself, one of Pussy Welles and the third of an old lady with thin lips and hard eyes. Mistress and mother. He picked up the photograph of Lomax, a younger Lomax, a studio potrait which was vaguely familiar – probably because it was the one which appeared on the dust covers of his popular books on natural history. An intelligent face but the intelligence inhibited by destructive self aware-ness. Thin lips turned down at the corners; a man unhappy with himself but contemptuous of his fellows. Under great stress he might be capable of anything, and suicide would be his ultimate escape.

Pussy Welles had been dead for ten days. Wycliffe felt unusually depressed, he had been involved from the beginning and there had been another death, but he had to admit that far from being able to offer proof of guilt he was still unsure in his own mind where the guilt lay. He told himself that the difficulty arose from the composite nature of the case as it presented itself; in part, and essentially, it was a series of events deliber-ately planned by the dead girl to relieve her boredom, to exact retribution or merely to demonstrate her power, but superimposed on this pattern was another, the product of expediency and fear. The difficulty was to separate the two. He was not even sure to which category of events Pussy's own death belonged. It was like a jig-saw puzzle in which a number of 'foreign' pieces had been substituted and you had to begin by weeding them out. There could be no doubt that Pussy Welles was the real criminal but it was equally certain that she had not herself performed all the criminal acts. The law was only interested in identifying her accom-plice and demonstrating his guilt. Lomax? Possibly. Young? He was her brother but did this tell in his favour or against him? In any event, he was a victim – how to explain that away? Mitford? Introspective, emotionally immature, under petticoat rule; perhaps nobody had paid enough attention to him. Ursula Barnes had said something about meeting him on the cliffs but it had been lost in the excitement created by her other news. Mitford must be remembered. Dampier? Wycliffe had to admit to a prejudice in his favour; of all the people who figured in the case Dampier was the only one with whom he felt able to achieve a common bond of either understanding or sympathy. But the fact remained that he was mentally able and physically crippled, a man unlikely to be restrained by the same sanctions which are effective with those who are either less intelligent or less frustrated.

Then there were the queers. Wycliffe was unable to take them seriously; for him they were a joke in bad taste. But he had an ingrained revulsion against homosexuality which no amount of objective argument could destroy. Reed was mean and he was prepared to believe that he was also vicious but it seemed extremely unlikely that Pussy Welles had ever made him a partner in anything.

He became aware that the light was fading, that he had been day-dreaming. The sky behind the church was flushed with the afterglow of sunset and soon it would be dark. He went downstairs and found Darley alone in the study; he was sitting at the dead man's desk going through those items which his subordinates had thought worth his attention.

'I take your point,' he said, 'Lomax was left handed.'

'What?' Wycliffe found this ability to resume a conversation exactly where it had been left off an hour ago, disconcerting. 'Oh, you mean the business of the paraffin test? I happened to notice that the other evening, he seemed to use his left hand for preference, then this afternoon I saw that the written material on his desk suggested left handedness.'

Darley nodded. 'He might still have used his right hand on the gun; many people who have a left handed tendency are almost ambidextrous.'

'Of course, but it would be interesting to know the extent to which he used his right hand. What about figerprints on the gun?'

'His own, quite a good set from the right hand, blurred as you would expect in firing two shots.'

Darley switched on the desk lamp and the twilight outside suddenly gave way to darkness. They could hear singing from the church, an Easter hymn:

> *Jesus lives! thy terrors now*
> *Can, O Death, no more appal us;*

'I would like your opinion on these.' He picked up a slim wad of papers, letters, written on sheets of different sizes and colours, all in the same neat, small hand. 'They're from Pussy Welles to Lomax and they go back six or seven years – to the time when he was still at the university and she worked there as a secretary.' He pointed to a length of blue ribbon on the desk. 'They were tied up with that – imagine it, in a man of his age! But they seem to settle our case.'

Wycliffe brought another chair into the circle of light and settled down to read. There were about two dozen letters spread unevenly over the period, presumably she wrote only when they were separated for more than a day or two and this was confirmed by phrases from the letters:

'since you've been away . . . ' 'I've missed you, especially at the weekend . . .' and 'I shall be home all Thursday evening so if absence has made you fonder . . .'

The earlier letters were full of affectionate regard, the young girl impressed and flattered by the attention of a distinguished older man.

> *You shouldn't apologize for writing often, surely you realize that I'm flattered by your interest . . .*

Later, written while she was on holiday in Cornwall:

> *If you must justify our relationship by precedents, remember that Beatrice was only fourteen when Dante found her. I am twenty-one!*
> *No! You never bore me with details of your work, I revel in being associated, even distantly, with anything creative . . .*

'He must have lapped it up, poor devil!' Wycliffe said. Darley was going through Lomax's other papers – drafts of articles, business letters, bank statements. He looked up with a tired grin. 'No fool like an old fool!'

Then the tone of the letters changed:

> *Really, Edgar, you can't expect to monopolize me. I know you would be the last to want me to feel that I had been bought by your presents, much as I appreciate and value them.*

A little later:

> *No, I do not mean that things are finished between us but I have never led you to believe that our*

relationship was or could be an exclusive one. You are very foolish to try to get consolation from drink, that will solve nothing and may cost you your job. Try to realize that you have not 'discovered a guilty secret of mine'. I have never tried to make a secret of my life and certainly do not feel any guilt. You must understand that in my own way, I too am rather a 'special person' and I have no intention of belonging to anybody.

Then there was a gap in the letters. When they resumed, Lomax had settled in Kergwyns and Pussy had married and was living with her husband in St Ives.

A woman pays for her mistakes, but in all honesty I must admit that I have nobody to blame but myself. When I think, dear friend, of what you offered me compared with what I now have! But there is no going back . . .

You can't imagine how I look forward to our little meetings but they make me sad for I cannot help but be reminded of how things might have been . . .

And then, on the day of the inquest on her husband:

I have never been so happy, it is like being reprieved from a life sentence! Thank you, thank you, thank you! I will make sure that you never have any regrets. But we must be circumspect, my dearest, that is what I find most difficult! When the coroner (pompous old fool!) expressed sympathy with the widow, I nearly laughed in his face! But we must be careful for the time being, there must be no hint of suspicion. What would I do if . . . ? There, I can't bring myself even to write of the possibility.

Another long gap, almost three years, then:

. . . you are welcome at the cottage now as always, it is childish of you to write. It is not I who have changed . . . You have become morbidly introspective and a source of concern to your friends . . . Sometimes I fear that you are developing a persecution complex. Perhaps you should get advice, I am sure that John will know a good alienist . . .

The last letter was dated two days before Pussy Welles died:

My Dear Edgar,
    You are becoming extremely tiresome in your persistence. I have always despised jealousy as the most futile of emotions. Either you have the courage to do something about it or you haven't. I have told you more than once that you have no special claim on me and your threats are merely ludicrous. By all means come to the cottage if you wish – Thursday evening will suit me – though I can't promise that you will be reassured.
                                                Pussy.

Wycliffe put down the little pile and sat back in his chair. Darley sat back too. 'Well? What do you think of them?'

Wycliffe seemed reluctant to talk, the letters had affected him strangely, his features registered only blankness and he regarded the inspector dully. 'I don't know what to think. That is the most incredible collection of documents I have ever come across.'

Darley was surprised. 'Incredible? I wouldn't say that; surely you've been telling me all the way through, what an extraordinary girl she was – these only prove you right. Utterly amoral, she got her kicks by manipulating people as though they were puppets which is more or less what you said about her.'

Wycliffe said nothing and Darley went on, 'In the end, one of her performers proves to be flesh and blood after all, and gets his own back. I can't say I blame him, although he's a murderer twice over.

'Isn't that how you see it?' he demanded when Wycliffe remained silent and inscrutably blank.

'I don't know.'

'But surely you agree that Lomax shot himself?'

'It certainly looks like it.' Wycliffe raised his hands in a gesture of bewilderment. 'But why?'

'Why? You ask that after reading those letters? The wretched man had lost his job, committed murder and goodness knows what else for this evil little baggage but instead of the reward he hoped for, he got the brush off. So he killed her, and you ask why, after all that, he committed suicide!'

'I suppose you are right.'

The inspector shuffled the papers on the desk impatiently. 'I'm sorry, sir, but I really can't understand your attitude.'

'So it's all over?'

'Yes, bar the shouting, and there won't be much of that. Nobody is very interested in a murderer who commits suicide, the great British public will feel that they've been done.'

'It seems such an unsatisfactory ending.'

Darley looked at him in astonishment. 'Unsatisfactory! But we aren't writing detective stories! This is for real!'

Wycliffe smiled. 'For real! – I shall remember that.'

He got up and moved towards the door. Darley watched him uneasily.

'I'll see you in the morning.'

The superintendent walked slowly back to the inn. The watchers had tired of their vigil for it was dark. There were few lighted windows, even on Sundays the villagers seemed to avoid the front of their houses and, in any case, most of the men were at the inn. As he entered the bar conversation faltered and died. They watched him and made way for him to reach the counter where Sylvie and the little rat-faced man were busy.

'How is he?'

Sylvie tossed her head. 'He's had some black coffee and he's getting dressed. I think he'll live.' She drew a pint of bitter, pushed it across to a customer, picked up the wet money and gave change. 'I've tidied up and I doubt if he'll notice if you don't tell him.'

'I won't,' Wycliffe promised. 'In fact, I'd say nothing to anybody of what happened last night or this afternoon.'

She grimaced. 'I know how to hold my tongue; I've had enough practice.'

'Good!'

After dinner he walked on the cliffs and watched the rain clouds creep in over the sea, shutting out the stars. Once more that night he found sleep through the devious pattern of one of Pussy's puzzles.

Rodent Operator and Musician, four and five. *Pied Piper!* Wycliffe was pleased with himself. That gave a *P* to start one across. *Small dog in leading strings?* That checked him for a while. Six letters. He thought of pup and he thought of pet but it was some time before he put them together: *Puppet* . . .

He heard the church clock begin to chime midnight but he was asleep before the twelve strokes had doled themselves out. Two or three times in the night he woke and found himself thinking about the case. His thoughts seemed unusually lucid which probably meant that his critical faculty was still asleep, but he felt peaceful and contemplative so that when he finally woke he wasn't surprised to find that he was on the brink of decision.

Half past six; rain with a wind behind it, driving water down the window panes. Since coming west he was getting to like rain. He got out of bed and stood looking out of the window. Below him, the backyard of the inn, stacked with barrels, glistening in the rain and surrounded by a high wall; beyond a stretch of gorse and heather to the cliff edge and the sea, but today his vision was bounded by the sheeting rain. Even so, by bringing his face close to the glass he could see the roofs of the bungalows in the lane.

'Bloody fool!' He muttered to himself, then he put on his dressing-gown and slippers and went downstairs.

It gave him a perverse pleasure to hear Darley's sleepy voice at the other end of the wire.

'I hope I haven't got you up.' He waited while Darley made certain unspecified preparations for a more extended conversation. 'About the two bullets fired from Lomax's gun – I want you to ask the ballistics people whether they can offer any evidence at all as to which was fired first, the one that went into the book or the one that killed Lomax . . .'

'So you still think it might be murder?'

'Perhaps, but never mind about that . . .'

'But surely it's impossible for ballistics to tell anything of the sort?'

Wycliffe was impatient. 'Ask anyway. Remember that the gun probably hasn't been fired for a very long time before this – if ever. And get on to them first thing. I don't want this balled up.' It never took long for Darley to ruffle his sunniest mood.

'And the letters – the letters from Pussy to Lomax – get them tested for prints . . .

'Anybody's, yours, mine, the dead man's, Pussy Welles', Uncle Tom Cobleigh's. Then I want them examined by a handwriting expert. Gordon Cleaver who used to work for the Home Office lives somewhere in this area – take them to him . . . Yes, you can take a specimen of her writing along if you like but I'm not questioning that she wrote them. I'm sure she did.

'And Darley . . . come and have lunch with me here.' He was pleased with himself; no doubt about that. Darley was impressed and mystified too. But he would look a damn fool if it all went wrong.

As he left the booth he could hear Sylvie in the kitchen and he went to get some coffee. She was hollow-eyed.

'You look tired; you're overdoing it.'

'You can say that again; he's been with me most of the night – after sympathy and you know what.'

'You don't have to put up with it.'

He watched her pour the coffee from the percolator into the cups.

'He's asked me to marry him.'

'And will you?'

'I could do worse, I suppose; this place could be a gold mine.'

He sensed that she was asking his advice and he thought of Mary, his own daughter, not much younger than Sylvie. He was deeply touched but there was no advice he could give her, the contexts were so different.

'Good morning, superintendent.' It was Young, early abroad, in pyjama tunic and trousers. He looked ill. But he was amiable and a little shamefaced. 'Sylvie told me you wanted to talk to me yesterday about poor Lomax. The fact is, I had the father and mother of a hangover – I expect you guessed. But if there's anything I can do now?'

'Two questions, Mr Young, that's all.'

Young took a crushed cigarette packet from his trousers pocket, picked out one, straightened it and lit up. 'Fire away!'

'The man you saw talking to Horner on the evening of his death was Lomax?'

'What do you think?'

Wycliffe nodded. 'Now, on the night of your car crash, you told the police that Lomax was in St Ives, though Lomax himself said that he was at home.'

Young raised his shoulders and grimaced. 'I know he was there; I saw him and I saw his car in the car park, not far from mine.'

'Ah! And when you went to fetch your car, did you notice whether or not his was still there?'

The innkeeper turned full face as he spoke. 'It was gone, the car park was empty.'

'So you've known all along?'

Young's eyes narrowed. 'Not *known*, superintendent, I had no proof.'

'And you did nothing.'

He stubbed out the butt of his cigarette. 'Once when I showed the slightest sign of stepping out of line, I was nearly killed in that smash. It taught me a lesson. A single unguarded remark about Arthur Horner, here in this bar, led to that in twenty-four hours.'

'So when I pressed you on Saturday night in front of Lomax, you went home and drank yourself into a stupor because you were scared?'

'I'm not denying it.'

'But there's nothing to be scared of now.'

'No.' Young agreed in a curiously level voice. 'As you say, there's nothing to be scared of now.'

'Well, thank you, Mr Young.' Wycliffe moved to the door, then turned back. 'It may interest you to know that there was a constable on duty here all Saturday night, so that the risk was not overlooked.'

Young's face was impassive. 'I've never had much faith in the police, superintendent, but thanks all the same.'

Chapter Eleven

Tuesday evening at Lomax's house, and another gathering of those who were known to have the strongest reasons for interest in Pussy Welles, dead or alive. This time there was no subterfuge, no attempt to cloak the purpose of the gathering in a socially acceptable guise; all of them knew why they had been asked to come and any doubts were dispelled by the place of their meeting. You can't make merry in a dead man's study, at least, not before he is decently buried. (Lomax was not buried, his body rested transiently in a refrigerated drawer at the county mortuary.) The same people would be there, except for Lomax himself, and Ricky Barnes would take his place.

A fine evening after two days of almost continuous drizzle, a waning moon and starlight. The Barneses parked their Mini in the square and walked back, arm in arm, very close, revelling in mutual self abasement and the cosy business of making it up. But Barnes was edgy, his wounds still raw. No-one answered the bell but the outside light was on and the door stood ajar.

'They said we should go in.'

There was no-one else about but the lights were on in the study and a wood fire blazed and crackled on the hearth. Somebody had arranged chairs and there was a table with drinks and glasses.

'I don't know why we had to come.'

Ursula was patient, as with a child. 'We didn't *have* to, darling, but it seemed a good idea. We might as well *know* what's happening; we have a right to that at least.'

Richard went to the drinks, poured himself a whisky and splashed soda.

'I don't suppose they'll mind,' Ursula said.

'I don't care a damn if they do!' He sipped his drink and wandered moodily round looking at the bookshelves. 'I've never been in here before – queer bird, Lomax. I wonder why he did it?'

'There was something very odd about him.'

Barnes laughed bitterly. 'I expect they said that about me – "I always thought he was a bit shifty – he didn't quite ring true if you see what I mean," – know-all bastards!' He stopped suddenly and faced his wife, 'You don't think they've got me here on false pretences? I mean there's still plenty they could charge me with . . .' His look was pleading, he seemed to beg for reassurance and she gave it, bolstering up his courage until he became aggressive again.

The bell rang and Ursula went to let in Alfred Mitford and Janice. They seemed surprised and put out and Barnes instantly concluded that it was because of him. Alfred sat on a fireside stool, hands clasped over his knees. Janice poured herself a gin; she was tense, excited, her movements were exaggerated and twice she spilt some of her drink down the front of her dress. 'This all seems very odd to me. I mean why are they throwing us together like this? What do they expect to gain by it?'

'I suppose they think we are entitled to some explanation,' Ursula said.

'Explanation!' Janice was contemptuous. 'This is a

police trap, my dear, and don't you make any mistake about it!'

'Trap? What for?' Barnes was anxious and she was flattered by his appeal to her.

'What for? To catch the murderer. They've let us think it was Lomax, that he committed suicide because he was guilty, but I heard on good authority that he was murdered . . . Poor Edgar!' She added as an afterthought, 'He never did anybody any harm.'

'I don't believe it!' In her anxiety to shield her husband, Ursula was too emphatic for good manners and Janice bridled.

'You believe what you like, but we shall see before the night is out. In any case, you've nothing to worry about, Ricky's been acquitted. The accused leaves the court without a stain on his character! Isn't that what they say? And you can't be tried twice for the same crime.'

'Janice!' Even Alfred was constrained to protest at his wife's indiscretion. 'You must be out of your mind.'

Janice laughed hysterically. 'I expect I am, and is it any wonder?' She looked at Ursula. 'You might as well know that I'd give a lot to be in your shoes.'

'In *my* shoes? I don't know what you're talking about, Janice.'

'You know they can't touch your husband, he's safe, but what about mine?'

Alfred groaned. 'For God's sake, Janice!'

Either the Dampiers didn't ring the bell or they weren't heard; they just walked in and their arrival served to distract Janice. Dampier made for one of the armchairs and never spoke until he was settled, it was as though he believed himself invisible until he opened his mouth. Erica seemed aware of the tension, she looked pale and haggard, but she smiled. 'I don't suppose this is going to be a jolly evening.'

'At least they've laid on something to drink,' Dampier said. 'Pour me a whisky, Alfred . . . No soda, just a dash of water, don't drown it . . . thanks, that's fine.' He tasted his drink and looked round with twinkling eyes; whatever the others might think, he was determined to get what enjoyment he could out of the evening. 'First time I've ever been here. It's not what I expected and yet it's Edgar, Edgar to the "T", sober, pompous and . . . what's the word? . . . fatuous.'

'John!' Erica protested mechanically.

'Well, that's what he was and we all know it, being dead doesn't alter that.'

'I wouldn't have said it was a very apt description of a murderer,' Barnes said, and he spoke with careful articulation like a man who is a little drunk and afraid of showing it. 'There must have been more to him than we thought.'

'Murderer?' Dampier was contemptuous. 'Edgar never murdered anybody, he wouldn't kill a chicken.'

'There! What did I tell you?' Janice seized on an ally.

But Dampier's mood was expansive, he swept on, 'By the way, Richard, I haven't said how glad we are to see you back in circulation. How does it feel?'

Barnes poured himself another whisky. 'I haven't had a chance to find out yet, the repercussions are only beginning.'

'Repercussions?'

'The University have offered me a Sabbatic term, you can guess what that means.'

'It means that they are sympathetic and want to help,' Ursula asserted.

'Nonsense! It's a broad hint and the opportunity to look for another job.'

Dampier fondled his beard; he seemed to take pleasure in its black profusion. 'I'm more concerned about who will take your place.'

'Take my place? Where?' Barnes was sharp, ready to take offence.

'Why, in gaol, of course!' Nervous laughter with Mitford looking disapproving, as though they were being sacriligious.

A minor commotion in the passage and Aubrey Reed came in, followed by Harvey Clemens. Reed stood for a moment, hands thrust deep into the pockets of his suede jacket; his eyes shone, he was excited. It occurred to Dampier for the first time, that he probably doped. 'Well? Where is everybody? Where's the superintendent?'

'Why don't you get yourself a drink?'

Reed poured gin, Clemens opened a bottle of ale. The church clock chimed and started to strike. Everybody listened and counted as though they didn't know the time already.

'Eight o'clock. Sounds close, doesn't it?' Clemens remarked. He looked round, 'Quite a party, aren't we? Like Christmas.'

'We could play games while we wait,' Reed said. 'So this is where the great man worked. I've never been in here before, have you?' He put the question, pointedly, to Mitford. 'But perhaps I shouldn't ask that, inviting a man to incriminate himself.'

Mitford flushed but said nothing. Janice went white.

A crisis was averted by the arrival of Mike Young; he blinked in the light, muttered a word of greeting then made quickly for a chair close to Dampier. 'What's all this about then?'

Dampier was gruff. 'What makes you think I know?'

Young looked round, saw that the others were drinking and poured himself a stiff whisky. 'Who's paying for the drinks?'

'No idea. I suppose we must be guests of the police.'

'Catch those bastards paying for anything.' He took a good pull at his whisky, then looked approvingly at what remained in his glass. 'A drop of the good stuff, anyway!'

When Wycliffe arrived the moonlight was still bright enough to fill the little courtyard with haunting and deceptive shadows. But no lemmings now. He let himself in, hung his coat in the passage and opened the glass door into Lomax's study. A change to see it full of people, who sat about, drinking, presumably chatting, a bright fire crackling away. A meeting of village notables at the home of one of them to organize a protest about something or other. Spoilation of the countryside, drains or re-rating.

Wycliffe sat with a little table in front of him, completing the illusion he was taking the chair. Only the silence measured tension. Nobody had even greeted him.

Dry, speaking with scarcely any inflexion, he thanked them for coming. Informal get together . . . no compulsion on anyone . . . nevertheless co-operation appreciated . . . Everyone present more or less directly concerned with events to be discussed . . . Inquiries had reached the stage when it seemed best to acquaint them with certain facts. Having heard what it was about, did anyone want to leave?

Almost tangible relief. Nobody for the way out.

'Good!'

Wycliffe looked from one to another of his audience slowly, deliberately, as though he wanted to memorize their faces, then he began to talk, so quietly and with so little emphasis that they had to listen carefully in order to follow him. He might have been a don conducting a seminar, fully in control of his subject, but too detached to employ oratorical tricks or to make any attempt to involve his hearers. He suggested that the personality of Pussy Welles was the key to the case and proceeded to offer them a character sketch.

'I have been told that she wanted power for its own sake, that she wanted it badly enough for it to have become an obsession. In such degree, this is not a common phenomenon even among men and, fortunately, it is very rare among women. But when it occurs, it can be more dangerous, for, in my experience, women have a pragmatic approach to morality and they are capable of showing scant respect for taboos which might restrain a man.

'Pussy Welles attempted to achieve her ends through the weapon of her sex. She needed men, but she also used them, seeking a complex satisfaction which had its physical component but derived mainly from the humiliation and servitude she was able to impose on her conquests and in the fear of exposure which she exploited. Where her sex was of little avail, she was quick to use other means.' His eyes rested momentarily on Aubrey Reed. 'Blackmail of one sort or another was her speciality but not usually for material gain and this was her strength.'

He talked on, dry, precise. What the Sunday newspapers would have done with the same material! But

Wycliffe never failed to grip his audience and not only because they were so deeply involved. He had the gift of riveting attention.

'When she was killed – murdered, it seemed – there was no shortage of eligible culprits. The most cursory investigation uncovered credible reasons why any one of you, or Lomax, might have killed her. What material clues there were pointed uncertainly to Barnes. He behaved foolishly and by demonstrably false statements, drew attention to himself, then, two apparently damning pieces of evidence precipitated his arrest. An anonymous letter led to the discovery that his pistol was the murder weapon and he was further implicated by the testimony of a woman whom Pussy Welles telephoned only a short while before she was killed. In that telephone conversation, Pussy Welles said that she was pregnant, that Barnes was the child's father and that he was with her discussing what to do. She also hinted that she felt at some risk and the telephone call was intended to ensure her safety.'

Wycliffe matched his finger tips together and studied them in silence. Richard Barnes sat, hunched in his chair, staring at the carpet, and Ursula reached out to place her hand over his. Dampier was restless. He seemed to be on the point of saying something but couldn't quite make up his mind. Suddenly he burst out.

'But this is incredible!'

Wycliffe stared at him, mild eyed. Dampier looked quickly at his sister and away again. 'You know quite well that on the afternoon of the day she died, Pussy told me that she was pregnant and that I was responsible.'

'Well?'

'She threatened me.' He seemed to challenge the superintendent to press him further.

Young was looking at him but it was impossible to judge his thoughts.

'With what?'

Wycliffe cut in quickly. 'You saw fit to keep this to yourself when it might have affected my attitude to Barnes if I had known of it.'

Dampier said nothing and he continued. 'However, it was of little consequence in the long run for I was far from convinced of his guilt. I felt from the beginning that this case had deeper roots, that the death of this girl was part of a pattern. If Barnes had killed her, then it was an intrusive incident, not part of the design.

'I had a number of reasons for coming to this conclusion and they will emerge as I go on. Even when I was compelled to arrest Barnes I continued the case on the assumption of his innocence. But if he was innocent, he had been "framed" and *Pussy Welles was a party to it.*'

Aubrey Reed had sat through the exposition so far with the air of a bored spectator. He lit one cigarette from another and from time to time, sipped his gin. Now he laughed contemptuously. 'I've nothing against Ricky Barnes, but surely, it would be easier to believe that he did it rather than to accept the fantastic notion that Pussy Welles helped to frame him for her own murder.' He turned to the others for support. 'I mean, it's an ingenious idea for a thriller but hardly credible in real life, is it?'

'Lot of nonsense!' Young muttered. He had already had two stiff whiskies and went for the decanter once more.

'What do you think, Mr Dampier?' Wycliffe enquired.

Dampier fingered his beard. 'I could believe almost anything of that girl, but planning her own murder and contriving a trail pointing to the wrong man – the imagination boggles!'

'What about suicide made to look like murder?'

'Ah! That, as they say, is a horse of a different colour.'

'*Did* she commit suicide?' Erica Dampier, strained and white.

'She would have needed an accomplice.' Alfred Mitford spoke for the first time.

Wycliffe turned his attention to Mitford and he shrank back in his shell, wishing that he had had the sense to keep quiet. 'She *had* an accomplice. There's no doubt about that.'

Mike Young was chuckling. Such an unusual phenomenon that everybody loooked at him.

'Mr Young?'

The innkeeper patted his face with a grubby handkerchief. 'It's only that I'd never thought of it – the possibility that Pussy committed suicide, I mean. It would be just her idea of a joke if she intended to do away with herself, to do it so as to cause a hell of a fuss and, my God, she succeeded!'

'And what about her accomplice?'

Young became suddenly wary. After a moment he said, 'Lomax committed suicide, didn't he?'

Janice Mitford had scarcely spoken, she had followed intently everything that passed, looking from one speaker to another apprehensively as though any one might say the thing she dreaded to hear. But now she seemed to have worked herself up to a pitch of almost uncontrollable indignation. 'You mean she killed herself? That she deliberately caused all this misery and anxiety for nothing?' Her voice rose; as with most hysterical women her excitement was a self propagating chain reaction, but Young cut her short. He was venomous, menacing.

'Shut your mouth, Janice Mitford! Whatever Pussy did or didn't do, she was a real woman which is more than can be said for you!'

She looked as though she had been slapped; then she stood up, gathering the shreds of her dignity. 'I'll not stay here to be insulted! Alfred!' But Alfred caught her by the arm and pulled her back to her seat.

'For God's sake sit down and be quiet!'

Wycliffe went on as if nothing had happened. He reiterated his belief that the deaths of Pussy Welles and Lomax were linked with Arthur Horner's and with Young's accident. 'Grown men don't usually fall over cliffs when they are out for a summer evening stroll; neither is it common for five gallon oil drums to fall off lorries on lonely country roads, late at night. That these things and two other violent deaths should happen within the circle of a dozen acquaintances is improbable to the point of impossibility.' He stopped, his eyes on Young who was after his fourth whisky. 'I shouldn't, Mr Young!' He tidied the papers in front of him as he spoke. 'If you are going to follow my argument you'll need a clear head.'

Young looked aggressive, shrugged and sat down. 'I suppose it's your whisky.'

Wycliffe smiled vaguely. 'To continue: at the time of her death Pussy Welles had almost completed a novel called, *God and Maggie Jones*.'

'A novel!' Exclamation from Richard Barnes who had seemed to take little interest in what was going on.

'A remarkable account of a girl, Maggie Jones, who enters into a sort of working partnership with God and between them they set out to play merry hell with the tight little community to which Maggie belonged.'

'Odd she never mentioned it to me,' Barnes said. He didn't explain that it seemed strange because he had bored her with his novel whenever the opportunity arose. He seemed yet to feel some obscure slight and Ursula looked at him sharply.

Wycliffe hesitated. 'In my opinion, it is an extremely clever novel, sometimes mischievous, penetrating and irreverent, but often cruel, vicious and frightening. There is no justice in it; the punishment never fits the crime but is always wildly excessive. One is reminded of the grotesque spite vented by Elisha on the children of Bethel, or some equally senseless atrocity. Often there is no offence at all, punishments are meted out with a sort of sadistic glee and sometimes it seems to be virtue itself which is pilloried. Certainly it is a book from an able though warped mind.'

Dampier adopted a rather patronizing manner, reasonable, judicial. 'I think I see your point. You are saying that Pussy Welles tried to give substance to her fantasy and that she put these inverted notions to work.'

Wycliffe said nothing and Dampier went on: 'I knew of her novel though the possibility that it was a sort of blueprint for action never occurred to me, but it would be in character and she was capable of bringing it off. It explains a lot.'

'I would like to manipulate people rather than ideas.' Barnes again, and everybody looked at him in surprise.

'That's what she said to me shortly before . . . before she was killed. She was talking about power and how she yearned for it. I suggested that in another incarnation she might like to be a general, and she said, "A general by all means, but only in wartime, peacetime generals are pathetic figures, children playing with rather stupid toys." '

'So she made her own war,' Dampier said. 'Getting back to the novel, doesn't it strike you as interesting that her partnership was with God rather than the devil? It suggests that she wanted to give her ideas – her actions if you are right – at least the colour of morality.'

Wycliffe shook his head. 'I disagree. I think her choice of God rather than the devil was her ultimate piece of cynicism. But whatever the intention, her book left me in no doubt that she had planned the sequence of events which led, at last, to her death though whether her death was part of the plan could be argued.'

Erica Dampier actually shivered. 'I've always known she was a *wicked* woman, she brought untold evil into this village.'

Wycliffe nodded. 'But no matter how wicked she was, she wasn't alone, she had an accomplice, someone equally culpable in law and the question for me has been – who? Who was her accomplice?' He let the question hang in the air and a new wave of disquiet seemed to ripple round the room.

Dampier smoked one of his cheroots, eyeing the superintendent through the smoke haze; Young, next to him, presented the good side of his face creating an illusion of disinterest by gazing into a far corner of the room. Ursula Barnes sat, legs together, feet tucked in, skirt pulled down – unassailable, but she stole frequent solicitous glances at her husband. He lay back in his chair, legs thrust out, prickly, aggressive. Gaol might have reversed the roles in that household and in the long run he might come to think it cheap at the price. Erica Dampier sat bolt upright, her hands fiddling with the clasp of her handbag like a rosary. Anxious virgin; if anything happened to her brother, she would turn Catholic and enter a nunnery. Good thing too, better than dogs. Aubrey Reed, cross-legged, nonchalant, watched the smoke spiral from his cigarette; Harvey Clemens seemed to doze, incapable of sustained attention. Janice Mitford, showing leg to her suspenders, rolled the little ball of her handkerchief but never took her eyes off Wycliffe. Alfred looked profoundly gloomy but it was impossible to judge the depth of his emotion. He avoided meeting anyone's eyes.

'Let me say at once,' Wycliffe went on, 'that I had little hope of answering my own question. But for Lomax's death, it may have remained unanswered.'

Was there an audible sigh? Certainly the tension evaporated.

'You mean that you accept his guilt?' – Dampier driven to probe but perhaps as relieved as the rest.

Wycliffe shrugged. 'I'm here to give you the facts, you must choose your own interpretation. Lomax can't be put on trial so there is no question of a conviction.

'From the beginning it seemed to me that each one of you had motive and, with one exception, opportunity to kill Pussy Welles. But I was convinced that her death must be viewed in the light of other, earlier crimes that involved her and an accomplice. This narrowed the field but it did not focus on any single person. As I saw it, the women were out – no woman could have sustained a partnership with Pussy Welles. By the same token, Reed and Clemens were hardly to be taken seriously as suspects and, in any case, it turned out that they had their own reasons for a bitter antipathy that excluded collusion.' Wycliffe looked straight at Reed, but Reed said nothing. Perhaps he thought that he was getting off lightly. 'And Barnes was out. He might have killed the girl but he couldn't have participated in crimes which took place before he came to the village. That left Dampier, Mitford, Young and Lomax. It rested between them. But Young was a victim – very nearly a dead one.'

'So then there were three.' Clemens, with unexpected awareness.

'Three,' Wycliffe agreed. He seemed to be sluggish, heavy. It was as though he wanted to damp down interest, draw off steam and, intentionally or not, he was achieving an almost hypnotic calm. Long gaps with only the sound of crepitating logs and the pulse of the grandfather clock.

The church clock chimed.

'A quarter past nine,' Janice Mitford said.

'There seemed no getting beyond that point. I had suspicions – suspicions strong enough to be called convictions – but no proof and a very poor prospect of getting any.'

'And the only proof you have now is that poor old Lomax conveniently killed himself.' Dampier shifted in his chair, impatiently, powerfully, making the castors screech.

Wycliffe shook his head. 'Not quite. There were pointers even before Lomax died. The police made routine inquiries into the antecedents of everyone connected with the case . . .'

A little flutter of concern which Wycliffe seemed not to notice.

'. . . and established that Lomax was intimately acquainted with Pussy Welles while she was a secretary at the Registry and he had his lectureship. A classic sugar daddy situation you might think, expensive presents and the rest, but he so completely lost his head over her that when she started to play him up he went to pieces and had to resign.'

'Edgar Lomax? – I don't believe it!' Unexpected display of loyalty from Janice Mitford.

'No fool like an old fool!' Clemens seemed to have a stock of hackneyed aphorisms that he felt bound to work off.

'And then,' Wycliffe went on, 'there was always the possibility that we might persuade Young to talk.' His eyes rested on the innkeeper who continued to stare at one corner of the room. 'He tells us now, that he saw Lomax talking to Arthur Horner near where he was killed, shortly before it was supposed to have happened. He also admits now, that Lomax was on the road ahead of him on the night he had his smash. If Lomax had lived, we might still have got this information from him.'

Dampier swung round to face Young. 'If you can say all this now, why couldn't you have said it when he was alive? Are you trying to pretend that you kept quiet to save Lomax's neck? If you are, you'd do well to think of a better one!'

'I kept quiet to save my own neck. I knew, but I couldn't prove a thing.'

'Rubbish! Bloody rubbish!'

Young was controlled but firm. He loooked Dampier straight in the eyes and spoke with a certain dignity. 'You believe what you like, Mr Dampier, but it was because once, when I'd had too much to drink and hinted something in front of Lomax, that I had my smash. That was why I was scared stiff when the super started to press me at your place last Saturday. It's all very fine to talk, but Lomax was a killer and he didn't need more than a suspicion.'

'I don't believe it!'

Wycliffe intervened. He produced an official looking envelope, opened it and took out a little wad of photostats.

'Perhaps these will change your view.' He passed the photostats to Dampier. 'They are letters from Pussy Welles to Lomax and they cover several years.'

Dampier put on a pair of heavy, horn-rimmed spectacles and began to read the letters.

'You will see that the more significant passages have been marked.'

At first, Dampier read casually as one compelled by courtesy to consider evidence for an argument patently absurd. But his manner changed. As he read he allowed ash to grow on his cheroot until it fell in a grey shower onto his jacket, unnoticed. The others watched in silence. Young, in particular, never took his eyes from the letters. Wycliffe drew complex doodles on the empty envelope and waited. Richard Barnes got up to put another log on the fire, raising a great shower of sparks from the embers. At last, Dampier took off his glasses and handed back the photostats. He was subdued, chastened. He made a gesture of acceptance, murmured an apology. 'How little we know each other!'

Wycliffe glanced round at the company. 'These are copies of private letters, but both the parties are dead and if any of you wish to see them, you may. You have seen that their contents caused Mr Dampier to change his view of the case.'

Nobody spoke and he collected the letters and put them back in the envelope.

A moment of silence then conversation broke out. Tongues were freed and wagged on the subject of Lomax's guilt. Janice Mitford and Reed with returning courage asked to see the letters.

'It's difficult to believe that it's all over,' Erica Dampier said to no-one in particular. 'We can go on almost exactly as we did before.'

'I still can't believe that Edgar . . . Of all the terrible things! He seemed such a mild man, wouldn't say "boo" to a goose.'

'A bachelor at a dangerous age,' Ursula Barnes pronounced, now firmly aligned on the side of marriage.

'He was a queer bird,' Clemens summed up. 'A queer bird.'

'His epitaph, poor devil!' Dampier said.

In the general relaxation Young poured himself another drink.

Chapter Twelve

'When did you first discover that she was your sister, Mr Young?' Wycliffe asked the question conversationally but it brought a silence as abrupt and complete as a gunshot.

Young's whisky spilt down over his shirt front; Wycliffe stood by his chair, looking down at him. 'Don't waste time making up stories, Mr Young, there's no point now, is there? No reason why people shouldn't know the truth. It's all over – just a few stray ends.'

Young still said nothing, he sipped his whisky and stared at the floor.

'She told you herself didn't she? Probably handed you that copy of her birth certificate, laughing, as though it had all been a good joke. When did it happen? The date on the certificate is a little while after your accident.'

'What about it?'

'That was when she told you – when you were in hospital?'

He nodded. 'I didn't believe it at first . . .'

'But she convinced you. All she had to do was to take off her sock. You knew about her deformed foot, didn't you?'

'Of course I knew about it, I was eight when she was born.'

'You never made any attempt to find her?'

'Not really. I wondered about her sometimes; wondered whether we had ever run into each other without knowing it. And all the time . . .'

'You were separated soon after she was born?'

'A few months. Our parents were both killed and there was nobody to look after us so we went into an orphanage. People want babies so she was adopted but I was there for a goodish while. Then I suppose you might say I struck lucky.'

The superintendent's manner was puzzling. His interest in the conversation seemed to be peripheral but he continued to probe. What was more surprising he appeared to be unaware of the interest he was creating. The proverbial pin might have escaped notice but not much else.

'I was puzzled why a girl like Pussy Welles should identify herself so completely with Cornwall and with this part of it in particular. From her late teens until she died she seemed to spend all the time she could here. When did you first meet?'

Young was gaining in confidence and he showed no reluctance to talk. 'When she was eighteen, down here on holiday. She came into the bar one lunch-time with a mixed bag of other youngsters.'

'You think she knew you then?'

'Looking back, I'm pretty sure she did. She made a dead set at me.' He put his hand to the injured side of his face. 'I didn't think much about it at the time, I was used to a bit of attention from the girls but this was different, she singled me out . . .'

'And then?'

He lit a cigarette before replying. 'You haven't been snooping round here for the past fortnight without finding that out. Whenever she was down we spent a lot of time together. I fell for her; leave it at that.'

'Until she married.' Wycliffe sipped a gin someone had passed him. 'That must have been a shock.'

'I couldn't believe it. I'd always assumed it would come to that between us. There'd never been anything . . . you understand – so far and no further.' He passed his hand over his forehead. 'Which surprised me a bit, I must admit because I had good reason to think she hadn't been so coy with others. Still, if that was how she wanted it, it was good enough for me.'

He drew deeply on his cigarette and watched the rising smoke from his lips. 'She was a witch! She wasn't long in persuading me that she'd been duped into marrying Arthur Horner and that if ever she got free of him we'd take up where we left off. And all the time she knew . . .'

Another version of Pussy Welles. Wycliffe listened and understood things that had puzzled him. Young spoke so quietly now that his voice hardly reached the others and they hadn't the temerity to come closer.

'Lomax was her cat's paw, her *creature*, besotted with her, ready to do anything – *anything*.' He looked up at Wycliffe, a caricature of a smile on his lips. 'But who am I to talk?'

'What about your car smash?'

'His doing – he was jealous, though God knows why. She came to see me in hospital several times and once, when I was getting better, she brought the certificate – as you said, treating it as a joke. I could have killed her then. "We're two of a kind now, brother," she said, "we're both freaks but I can cover mine up and you can't." ' He broke off suddenly. 'Do you believe me?'

'I believe you,' Wycliffe said.

'By Christ! I wouldn't blame you if you didn't.

Sometimes when I think of her I can hardly believe she was real.'

'Why did Lomax kill her?'

He shrugged. 'You've seen the letters. She drove the poor sod beyond endurance.'

'Is that all?'

'All?'

'All you've got to tell me.'

Young looked puzzled, a little apprehensive. 'I suppose so. I don't know what you mean.' He hesitated. 'After Pussy was gone, I felt safer from Lomax, she was the brains and the *guts*.' He laughed. 'I even had a notion to get a bit of my own back, I nipped into his shed one night and mixed rat poison with the food he gives his lemmings.'

'When was this?'

'I did it more than once.'

'But you didn't kill him?'

'Kill him? He committed suicide!'

Wycliffe said, 'No, Lomax didn't commit suicide, he was murdered. There's no doubt about that.'

'Murdered!' From Erica Dampier.

'There! What did I tell you?' Almost a scream of triumph from Janice Mitford.

Wycliffe held up his hand. 'Lomax was murdered, Mr Young.'

The innkeeper was looking once more at the far corner of the room. Animation which had brought some life to his features a few minutes before, vanished, leaving him sullen, inscrutable. 'All right, if you want to tell fairy tales, I can't stop you.'

Wycliffe perched himself on the arm of Young's chair. 'Two bullets were fired in Lomax's study that night; one killed him and the other bedded itself in a book across the room. Of course, it was possible that not having used the gun for years, he wanted to make sure that it was in working order. In which case the bullet that killed him would have to be the second one fired. Experts will testify that although they can offer no *proof* they are of the opinion that it was the first bullet which killed Lomax and the second which bedded itself in the book. The gun was substantially corroded when it was fired and the interference with the rifling on the bullet due to rust, is significantly greater on the bullet that killed him. Similar confirmatory evidence is given by the cartridge cases.

Dampier was dissatisfied. 'But why should anybody fire twice if the first shot killed him? Just a greater risk of drawing attention.'

Wycliffe nodded. 'The murderer wanted to make sure that the death would be treated as suicide and he knew enough to realize that the police might apply the paraffin test. After shooting him therefore, he placed the gun in Lomax's hand and fired it a second time ensuring not only prints but powder marks as well. Of course, the police applied the test and found the powder marks on his right hand.'

'On his *right* hand?'

'You are going to say that Lomax was left-handed – he was, as far as writing is concerned but to what extent he was ambidextrous, I don't know.'

'He held cards in his right hand and played with his left,' Dampier said.

Wycliffe continued to stare at Young as though he expected enlightenment through attentive observation. Young was on edge, he darted glances here and there round the room, like a bird seeking a possible way of escape. 'You're talking bloody nonsense in my opinion,' he said at last, 'but if Lomax was murdered it wasn't by me. I left Dampier's place before half past ten, cashed up and went to bed.'

'But you got up again, Sylvie heard you.'

'Did she now? Well, if you must air my affairs in public, you might as well know that I went down to get a bottle of whisky from the cellar to get pissed – which I did.'

'You went out. Sylvie heard you undo the bar of the back door.'

'She was mistaken. What she heard was the bar on the cellar trap.' He seemed to be gaining rather than losing confidence. 'Anyway, how could I get out of the place without being seen by your bloody copper? Tell me that.'

'Over the back wall.' Wycliffe answered so promptly that Young was shaken. 'Then you circled the village over the moor and came into Lomax's by the road. At least, that's what you could have done.'

The innkeeper laughed. 'Could have done, might have done – you're wasting your time. The fact is, I didn't!'

'You were seen,' Wycliffe said.

'What's that?'

'I said that you were seen.'

The crucial moment. Wycliffe was strung up to the highest pitch of tension, his whole being concentrated on saying the right thing with the right inflexion, leading Young to the moment of truth and this was it. He had just gambled although to the others he seemed to speak casually; he seemed relaxed.

'Mitford saw you climbing over the wall, didn't you?' He turned to Mitford.

Mitford studied the tips of his toes. His reply was

barely audible but it was, 'Yes'. Then he added in a stronger voice, 'I was standing at my garden gate, in the shadow, smoking a cigarette before going to bed.'

Wycliffe knew a tremendous surging wave of relief but the others seemed not to notice anything. Even Young was buoyant.

'Trust you to be where you're not bloody well wanted. I suppose she turned you out of bed again!' He lit another cigarette. 'Anyway, it doesn't prove anything.'

'It proves that you're a liar and in a murder case a man is a fool to lie unless he has something to cover up.'

'I admitted poisoning the lemmings.'

Wycliffe nodded. 'So you did.'

The superintendent knew that a plainclothes sergeant was just outside the window, that Inspector Darley was standing in the corridor on the other side of the glass door, that six uniformed men were strung out round the house. All this in case Young made a break for it. They had him marked as a violent man. And Wycliffe sat on the arm of his chair, close enough, just in case . . . The church clock chimed, then began to strike. Everybody counted – ten.

Wycliffe took the photostats of the letters from his pocket and weighed them in his hand. 'You didn't ask to see these just now.'

Young looked up momentarily. 'No.'

'You already knew what was in them.'

'How could I know?'

Wycliffe spoke patiently, reasonably, as to a child. 'When I asked you why Lomax killed her, you said, "You've seen the letters. She drove the poor sod beyond endurance." '

'What of it? I've got imagination the same as the next man and I knew her.'

'The originals have been tested for fingerprints.'

'So?'

'None of those letters dated after Lomax's arrival in Kergwyns have his prints on them.'

'He must have handled them with gloves on.' Sneer.

'Why?'

'How the hell should I know?'

'You must admit that it's odd.'

'All right, it's odd.'

'There's something even odder: those letters were examined by a handwriting expert . . .'

'You're going to say she didn't write them?'

Wycliffe shook his head. 'No, she wrote them.' He chose one of the photostats and handed it to Young. 'Read that one.'

Young did as he was told or appeared to do so. 'Well?'

'What do you think of it? She is apparently thanking Lomax for killing her husband.'

The innkeeper shrugged. 'She was a fool to write it and he was a bigger one to keep it.'

'You noticed the date?'

'Between five and six years ago.'

'Yes. But the experts are prepared to swear that the original of this letter and of all those dated subsequently, were written within the past eight or ten weeks. They can tell by the ink.'

'Big deal! But it's nothing to do with me.'

Young had adopted a jaunty air but it was wearing thin. Every now and then he shifted nervously in his chair, barely controlling, it seemed, an impulse to violence. But he did control it.

Wycliffe thrust the photostat under his very nose. 'I

think this *is* to do with you. The original of this letter and of two others have your prints on them. You were careful but not careful enough. Your sister set up Lomax's death as she had previously set up her husband's and in both instances you were the executioner. She knew that he had kept a few letters of hers and where he kept them; she knew too that he had a gun. After you killed him with his own gun, you added a few more to the pathetic collection of her letters which now branded him as a murderer and as her accomplice, making his suicide not only credible but almost inevitable.'

Young gesticulated, protested, determined to stem the flood of accusation but Wycliffe rested a hand on his shoulder and spoke quietly but with such unmistakable menace that Young quailed as though before an expected blow. 'You will be quiet until I have finished, then you can talk as much as you like – if you still have anything to say.'

From that moment they all knew that Young would not resort to violence. He was afraid. Wycliffe continued in a voice like silk.

'Your sister did not live to see the outcome of her planning. You had murdered her as she intended that you should. You were her pawn, her *creature* – the word was yours – in that as in all else. She was wicked and intelligent while you are wicked and a fool!'

Wycliffe stood up and turned his back on the wretched man. There was no stirring of sympathy for Young but at that moment the room was almost equally antagonistic to the superintendent. He was like a circus trainer with a miserable animal at the end of a big whip.

But the whip was his personality.

He sat himself once more by the little table. 'It is

impossible to see clearly into the mind of the girl you killed. She wanted power, certainly, but more than anything she was possessed by an insatiable desire for sensation, a sensualist, a hedonist, she discovered as others have done that the appetite grows with what it feeds upon. The common experiences of life were miserably inadequate to the titillation of her emotional palate so she decided to create situations, to dramatize reality. Egocentric, narcissistic as she was, other people's feelings, even their lives were expendable in her pursuit of perverse and elusive satisfactions. Indeed, her schemes had to be destructive of the welfare and peace of others for only in this way could she appease her envy and express her contempt. Always thumbs down for the loser! Of course, she failed. There can be no success in the denial of the social nature of man. Dampier said of her: "The best that she knew was a mood of feverish excitement which always and quickly yielded to disappointment. She could not be satisfied, it was not in her nature."

'You may think as I did that this was a possible recipe for suicide.'

He looked slowly round at the half circle of faces. In the silence a wind stirred outside, grew and rattled the windows, then died away. Soon it would rain.

'But it would have been out of character for her to do anything so straightforward. She would be at great pains and contrivance in her final production. She would be murdered and in circumstances that would cast the net of suspicion wide.

'How did she set about it?' He addressed the question to Young who looked up, seemed about to speak then shook his head.

'Never mind! The broad outline is clear. Just now,

you called her a witch; you said that you could have killed her when she presented you with her birth certificate, when she taunted you with your disfigurement.'

'So I could! I wish I had!' His voice was scarcely more than a whisper.

'But you didn't. Instead you tried to keep out of her way. The whole village observed the change and put varying interpretations on it. But you were not allowed to escape entirely, she knew more than enough to keep you dangling – and you knew that she was reckless – capable of risking her own security to destroy yours. So you continued to provide her with a house, you did whatever little menial tasks she demanded of you, you came when you were called.

'And you were called on that Thursday night, sometime between nine and half-past. *Dampier saw you when he was leaving.*'

The others were merely spectators now, as little likely to interrupt as the audience at a play. Wycliffe and his victim seemed to be isolated from them, unaware of their existence.

'I don't know what exactly happened in that encounter between brother and sister but I can guess a good deal; certainly you learned for the first time, the truth about your car smash. Until then, you had been foolish enough to believe it an accident. That night you were given a circumstantial account of how she had driven to Kitt's Corner, parked her car beyond it, waited for the headlamps of your car, then released the oil over the road. She stood the drum in your path so that you would be certain to brake and swerve. The oil, she obtained from Mitford's garage.'

Young looked at the superintendent as though

mesmerized; no attempt now to avert the injured side of his face. 'You knew that?' His voice was distorted with emotion, he seemed to be near to weeping, overcome by self-pity. 'My God! Can you believe it? Her own brother!'

'So you killed her to even the score.'

Young made a gesture, vague, evasive, but said nothing.

'You will be charged with the murder of Lomax, make no mistake about that. If what happened that night with your sister is in any way an extenuation of the crime, you would be a fool not to use it. You went to her cottage that evening, the murderer of Arthur Horner – a crime that could never be proved against you. You came away having killed your sister and with her blueprint for murdering Lomax . . .'

Young began to speak; he was not answering any question, nor was he challenging or denying the accusations against him. In a way he was not responding to any external stimulus, he spoke to relieve an inner tension which had mounted beyond endurance. A violent man, but weak; now that violence had failed, he cracked. At first words came with difficulty, there were gaps when it seemed that the flow might fail altogether but slowly his voice gathered strength and he achieved greater fluency.

'It was about a quarter past nine and the house was all lit up. As I rang the door bell I heard her start the record player upstairs and when she let me in the music was so loud I could hardly hear what she said . . .' He raised a hand to his ear as though the sound still troubled him. 'She gave me an envelope and told me to keep it safe, otherwise it might do me a lot of harm. I couldn't make her out; she was excited, feverish, I'd never seen her like it before. I asked her if she was ill and she laughed. "No, I'm not ill but I'm going to die tonight." Of course I didn't know what she was talking about.'

He stared at the floor. Perhaps he was seeing again the girl in the cornflower blue dress living out the last minutes of her life. As he told his story Wycliffe gathered intense visual impressions, almost as though he watched the actual events from behind an impenetrable screen, cut off, incapable of intervention. The girl, infected with a madness bordering on ecstasy, transported by the illusion of power, setting on foot great events; the man, disfigured, sullen, scared, utterly at a loss, conscious only of standing on the brink of disaster.

'She was mad! Insane!'

She goes to a little cabinet. 'Do you want to die, Mickey?'

No answer but she has a gun levelled at him. 'You think I wouldn't do it but I tried once and nearly succeeded. You knew too much about me and you were becoming a bore . . .'

The music was drowning his senses, he couldn't concentrate but she was telling him about the night of his accident. Accident! She told her story as if it was a fairy story told to a child and he accepted it with the same childish blend of incredulity and belief, horror and fascination.

'Miraculously, you survived, then I realized it didn't matter. You were such a mouse, you would always do as you were told.' She came closer. 'And you will do, won't you, brother dear? If not, I'll shoot first you, then myself, which isn't at all as I planned. Answer me!'

'Yes.' A strangled ejaculation.

She laughs. 'I knew you wouldn't disappoint your sister.' She looks at her watch. 'Time for the telephone calls; everything to the minute.'

Two telephone calls which mystify him. All the time he is forced to sit so that she can see him from the little porch where the telephone is; all the time she has her gun at the ready. First she speaks to Elsa Cooper then to Barnes. All the time the music fills the little cottage and he is hard put to follow what she is saying but one fact is driven home.

'Is it true that you are pregnant?'

She smiles, the same smile that once captivated him. 'Oh yes, that's true enough.'

'And is Barnes the father?'

She laughs. 'They'll never know and neither will you.' Serious again, business-like. 'Time is short! Barnes will be here in a quarter of an hour and he mustn't find you.'

Now the real nightmare. She gives him his instructions, clear, concise; she produces a second gun – an automatic – and gives it to him. 'Remember! The automatic belongs to Ricky, the pistol to Edgar. Don't get it wrong.' Calm now, cautionary, a mother sending a dull child on an errand. Mickey, Ricky, Edgar – they might all be children playing games.

'Now!' She is six feet away, facing him, her pistol still on him. 'Now!'

Still like a child he wails, 'I can't.'

Upstairs the tempo of the music changes. He has no ear for music, no knowledge, but the chorus of voices is a lament of infinite sadness.

'Now!' She takes a step closer. 'I shall count down from five, and I shall fire if you have not . . . Five . . . four . . . three . . .'

She slips to the floor as though in a faint. He has not heard the sound of the shot, is unconscious of having pulled the trigger but she is dead, crumpled on the floor at his feet and he is standing over her with the gun in his hand. The music has stopped. Utter silence.

His first emotion is neither panic nor remorse but anger; anger that he has been tricked. He longs to injure her and there she is, at his mercy. He stoops, rips off her shoe, pulls up her dress, fumbles with her suspenders, tears off her stocking. There! My God! that will humiliate her! Let them find her like that! Then fear and prudence take over and he follows instructions. Just in time. Christ! The door bell! He is through the kitchen, through the little garden and out on to the moor. Barnes, the fool! He has her shoe and stocking stuffed in his pocket.

'So you see, I was driven to it. It was her or both of us.' (I couldn't help it, sir.) Immaturity without innocence.

They seemed to be awaking from sleep and a disturbing, haunting dream. Outside the rain had arrived, driven in from the sea by a violent squall, it beat against the window panes.

Wycliffe stirred himself, emerging slowly from the final pathetic drama conceived in the mind of the dead girl and recreated in the halting phrases of her killer.

'And Lomax?'

He put the question with infinite reluctance. Enough is enough.

Young shivered as though from a sudden chill. When he spoke, he was peevish, petulant, hard-done-by. 'She promised me that I would be safe, that they couldn't possibly suspect me, but she lied and she knew she was lying . . .' He sighed. 'The envelope she gave me – in it there was a letter to me. "You are safe now," she said, "as I promised – *except for Lomax . . .*" ' He passed a hand wearily over his brow. 'All the plan was there, the letters, and I had the gun. I decided not to do anything, to take the risk; then they weren't satisfied with Barnes. You didn't believe he did it and you seemed suspicious of me. That night at the Dampiers' I knew you were after me and Lomax was there. If she was telling the truth, all he had to do was speak . . . I couldn't take the risk after all. *She knew what would happen!* The words came in a hiss of venomous hatred.

'Are you willing to make a statement?'

Young nodded. 'Anything . . . get it over.'

Chapter Thirteen

Another Thursday evening and Wycliffe was back with his wife in their Exeter flat. Although it was dark they hadn't bothered to draw the curtains so the city lay mapped in lights, stretching to the horizon. He thought it beautiful but knew that he would change it if he had the chance for one of those bungalows in the lane that led to the sea at Kergwyns. The cathedral clock chimed distantly and struck ten. Three weeks ago at this time Ricky Barnes was ringing the doorbell at the cottage and getting no answer while Mike Young was stealing out the back way on to the moor. Puppets still though their puppeteer was dead. She lay, shot through the heart, a red stain seeping through the material of her cornflower blue dress. Now Young was dead; he had contrived to hang himself in his cell the day after his arrest, so there would be no trial. The case had left a deeper impression on the superintendent than any in his experience for he too had danced to the dead girl's tune, another puppet on a string. And because of it Lomax had died, poor deluded Lomax who wouldn't hurt a fly.

The Deputy had shrugged his immaculately tailored shoulders. 'But my dear fellow! It's an occupational hazard . . .'

One bright spot: a letter from Sylvie, written in erratic spelling with a temperamental ball-point pen: *In*

his will he left me everything . . . He must have meant it
about marrying me . . . He was weak but he wasn't all bad
. . . They say I shall have to put in a manager. If you and
Mrs Wycliffe want a holiday down here . . . it will be on
the house . . .

Helen, his wife, knew all about the case but they
hadn't spoken of it for a long time. Now she took the
risk. 'Charles, who killed her cat?' No need for explanations, she didn't have to introduce the topic, it was still
so much in their minds.

'Young, it was one of the little jobs she gave him to
do.'

'When she was planning her own death.'

'I suppose so.'

Silence for a while then Helen started again. 'Charles,
about the crosswords . . .'

'What about them?'

'I finished them yesterday.'

'Good for you.'

She hesitated, then took the plunge, 'It's all there,
Charles, her confession, if you like to call it that, though
it's more like an advertisement.'

'What are you talking about?'

'There are fifteen crosswords and if you arrange them
in the right order there is a simple code.'

'A code?'

'Yes. The solutions to the first clue across in each
case and to the third one down, taken together give
thirty words and those words are a message. It's
telegraphic but it's intelligible; I've written it out.'

'Switch on the light.'

Intelligible all right, telegraphic, certainly, but the
truth about four violent deaths, four purposeless deaths.

His wife tried to fill the silence. 'Certain words and

names struck me – they seemed too much of a coincidence – Pussy – Arthur – Young – lemmings . . . I mean, taken together . . .'

Taken together, the final cynicism, the ultimate cocking of the snook.

REAL HUMAN PUPPET THEATRE INVOLUNTARY ACTORS STARRING KILLER YOUNG BREATHLESS EXPLOITS INCLUDE DEATH DIVING ARTHUR SISTER MURDER FAKED SUICIDE SUPPORTING LEMMINGS SPECTACULAR AUTOMOBILE SMASH THRILLS MOTIVATION ANIMATION PRODUCTION BY PUSSY.

Punctuation was scarcely needed but Helen had written out a punctuated version: *Real human puppet theatre. Involuntary actors. Starring Killer Young. Exploits include death diving Arthur, sister murder, faked suicide. Supporting lemmings. Spectacular automobile smash. Thrills! Motivation, animation, production by Pussy.*

Wycliffe walked to the window. 'I might have known she would leave nothing to chance. Nobody must miss the point, but I did.'

'She must have been mad!'

'Her brother called her a witch and she was certainly the wicked witch in this fairy tale.'

THE END

WYCLIFFE AND THE DUNES MYSTERY
by W. J. Burley

Cochran Wilder had disappeared fifteen years ago while on a walking holiday in Cornwall. Recently released from a psychiatric hospital after conviction on charges of indecent assault, he had been a serious embarrassment to his MP father. And now, after several years, his body had been found, buried in the dunes.

Wycliffe suspects the involvement of six people, now well-established figures in the Cornish community. As teenagers they had been spending an illicit chalet weekend, right where the body was found. All are disturbed by Wycliffe's questioning, but then a second murder is committed, and the investigation takes on a new urgency.

'Good classic detection'
Sunday Telegraph

0 552 14221 2

WYCLIFFE AND HOW TO KILL A CAT
by W. J. Burley

The girl was slim and young, with auburn hair splayed out on the pillow. Wycliffe almost believed her asleep rather than dead – until he saw her face. Although death was by strangulation, someone had smashed her face in *after* she was dead. She lay in a sordid room in a seedy hotel down by the docks, but her luggage, her clothes and her make-up all indicated she was more expensive and classier than her surroundings.

Superintendent Wycliffe was officially on holiday, but the case fascinated him and he had to find out who she was, why she was lying naked in a shabby hotel room why she had a thousand pounds hidden under some clothing, and above all, why she had been 'murdered twice.

As he began to investigate, he found there was too much of everything about the case – too many suspects, too many motives, and too many lies.

0 552 14117 8

A SELECTED LIST OF CRIME NOVELS
AVAILABLE FROM CORGI BOOKS

☐ 13232 2	WYCLIFFE AND THE BEALES	W. J. Burley	£3.99
☐ 14264 6	WYCLIFFE AND THE DEAD FLAUTIST	W. J. Burley	£3.99
☐ 14268 9	WYCLIFFE AND THE TANGLED WEB	W. J. Burley	£3.99
☐ 14109 7	WYCLIFFE AND THE CYCLE OF DEATH	W. J. Burley	£4.99
☐ 13689 1	WYCLIFFE AND DEATH IN STANLEY STREET	W. J. Burley	£3.99
☐ 14267 0	WYCLIFFE AND THE FOUR JACKS	W. J. Burley	£3.99
☐ 13435 X	WYCLIFFE AND THE QUIET VIRGIN	W. J. Burley	£3.99
☐ 14266 2	WYCLIFFE AND THE SCAPEGOAT	W. J. Burley	£3.99
☐ 12805 8	WYCLIFFE AND THE SCHOOLGIRLS	W. J. Burley	£3.99
☐ 14269 7	WYCLIFFE'S WILD-GOOSE CHASE	W. J. Burley	£4.99
☐ 13436 8	WYCLIFFE AND THE WINSOR BLUE	W. J. Burley	£3.99
☐ 13433 3	WYCLIFFE IN PAUL'S COURT	W. J. Burley	£3.99
☐ 12804 X	WYCLIFFE AND THE PEA-GREEN BOAT	W. J. Burley	£3.99
☐ 14265 4	WYCLIFFE AND THE LAST RITES	W. J. Burley	£4.99
☐ 14117 8	WYCLIFFE AND HOW TO KILL A CAT	W. J. Burley	£3.99
☐ 14115 1	WYCLIFFE AND THE GILT EDGED ALIBI	W. J. Burley	£3.99
☐ 14221 2	WYCLIFFE AND THE DUNES MYSTERY	W. J. Burley	£3.99
☐ 14437 1	WYCLIFFE AND THE HOUSE OF FEAR	W. J. Burley	£3.99
☐ 14116 X	WYCLIFFE AND DEATH IN A SALUBRIOUS PLACE	W. J. Burley	£3.99
☐ 14295 6	A CLEAR CONSCIENCE	Frances Fyfield	£4.99
☐ 14043 0	SHADOW PLAY	Frances Fyfield	£4.99
☐ 14174 7	PERFECTLY PURE AND GOOD	Frances Fyfield	£4.99
☐ 13840 1	CLOSED CIRCLE	Robert Goddard	£5.99
☐ 13839 8	HAND IN GLOVE	Robert Goddard	£5.99
☐ 13982 3	A TOUCH OF FROST	R. D. Wingfield	£4.99
☐ 13981 5	FROST AT CHRISTMAS	R. D. Wingfield	£5.99
☐ 13985 8	NIGHT FROST	R. D. Wingfield	£4.99
☐ 14409 6	HARD FROST	R. D. Wingfield	£5.99